ONE SAVAGE UNION

A DARK MAFIA ROMANCE

CRIMSON BONDS
BOOK ONE

LOUISE LENNOX

AFROCHANT

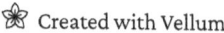 Created with Vellum

BLURB

I was a rising star—a concert pianist with the world at my feet.

Then my mother died... and took the truth with her.

Now I'm bound, body and fate, to Rocco Fieri—

a ruthless mafia heir who deals in secrets and blood.

He says I'm his.

The key to his family's power.

The woman who will wear his ring, bear his name, and kneel at his feet.

He rescued me from his sadistic cousin... but don't mistake that for mercy.

Rocco doesn't save—he claims. And what he claims, he owns completely.

I was raised to fight.

To sacrifice.

To never surrender.

But Rocco doesn't play fair.

He touches like a sinner and commands like a god—

breaking down every wall I built to survive.

Now I'm trapped in a marriage I never wanted,

at the center of a blood feud I never asked for.

And the most dangerous part isn't the war outside...

It's the war he ignites inside me.

One Savage Union is a dark mafia romance featuring a forced marriage, a possessive antihero, a brilliant and defiant heroine, and all the heat, violence, and emotional torment you crave. Includes BDSM themes, deadly secrets, a shattered legacy, and a guaranteed HEA that scorches before it soothes.

Read responsibly—Rocco will ruin you.

NOTE FROM AUTHOR

Parts of this book were previously published in my Kindle Vella Story, "Violent Ascension," under my now-defunct pen name, Georgia Blake. It has been remastered (TOTALLY) into the Happy Black Romance Novel it was always meant to be. I hope you love it!

Also....

This book contains triggers surrounding violence, parental death, light BDSM, and racism. Please read responsibly.

Enjoy!

To K,
My writing partner in crime.
I love you, babe!

"I am no bird; and no net ensnares me: I am a free human being with an independent will."
— *Charlotte Brontë, Jane Eyre*

PROLOGUE
ROCCO

For twenty years, I've waded through rivers of blood, left traitors smoldering in ash, and carved my name into the bones of enemies—to earn the power that comes with being Consigliere of the Romano Crime Family.

Betrayal stopped surprising me a long time ago—it's the currency we trade in.

But nothing—and I mean nothing—compares to the level of fucked up I've uncovered in the last forty-eight hours.

Two days ago, my uncle, Don Thomasso Romano, sent me to New York on a fact-finding mission. A whisper reached his ear: there was a rat among us. One of our gun shipments vanished from our docks in Chicago and ended up on the streets of New York with the Colombians.

Theft happens, but this one? It stank of betrayal.

Clean timing. Inside knowledge. No sign of struggle. It had our fingerprints all over it—just not the right hands.

And the Colombian Cartel isn't that stupid or that smart.

My orders were simple. Find the rat. Kill the rat. Make a spectacle of it so the rest of the family remembers what disloyalty costs.

I had to move carefully—New York isn't our turf, but stealth fits me like a second skin.

After kidnapping and torturing a few unfortunate souls, I managed to identify from the security cameras at our docks-I didn't find a rat.

I found a fucking snake.

Leo Romano.

The Don's son. My cousin. Blood of my blood.

He planned the heist. Funded it and pulled it off with a crew of mercenaries he'd been stockpiling like weapons, right under our noses for the past three months. And he didn't just steal from the family. He's desecrated the sacred oath of "la familia" and made a mockery of the blood that built our empire.

Once the informants used their last ragged breath to whisper his name, rage ignited inside me—pure, primal, and blinding. I wanted to find Leo and gut him like the scavenging bottom-feeder he is. No questions. No ceremony. Just justice—swift, sharp, and final.

But I'm not the Don.

And Leo's not my son.

So, today, I do what a Consigliere does—I bring the truth to the throne.

Adjusting the lapels of my black Tom Ford suit, I inhale once, steady and cold, before knocking on the polished mahogany door.

"Come in," Thomasso's voice calls, deep and even from his office.

I step inside—and find the bane of my fucking existence.

Leo

He's lounging against the wall beside his father's desk like he owns the place. He looks like rot wrapped in designer wool, oozing arrogance from every pore. His sneer is sharp enough to cut glass—and twice as toxic.

"Well, look who graced us with his presence," Leo slithers, voice slick with venom. "The crown prince of nothing. Tell me, cousin... how does it feel wearing a crown that doesn't belong to you?"

The poison in his voice isn't new, but today it seeps deeper—because now I know what fuels it. It's not jealousy. It's entitlement—warped into arrogance and flung like a blade by a traitor who truly believes he should be Don.

The delusion would be pathetic if it weren't so fucking dangerous.

I step to him—slow and deliberate—until we're nearly chest to chest, close enough that he can feel my calm like a blade at his throat.

"Feels lighter than betrayal," I say, voice like ice. "Funny how easy it is to wear what you earned."

I reach out, almost casually, and adjust the collar of his expensive jacket—just enough to remind him I could just as easily snap his neck.

Leo's smirk falters, his jaw tightens. He's not used to being touched without it leading to blood or surrender. That flicker of unease? I pocket it—ammo for later.

Before either of us can move further, Thomasso's voice cuts through the room, calm but laced with command.

"Enough."

We both turn. He's still by the bar, swirling his gin, but his eyes are locked on us—sharp, unblinking.

"I won't have my blood tearing each other apart in my office like rabid dogs," he says coolly.

"If either of you steps out of line, I'll bury the problem—family or not," Thomasso says, voice like steel wrapped in silk. His gaze doesn't waver. "And Leo... watch your mouth when you speak to Rocco. He's earned more in this family than you ever have. I've let your disrespect slide for too long."

He sets his glass down with a soft click, the sound final as a gunshot.

"Now, Get out. We're done for today."

Leo straightens, jaw tight. "But—Father—"

"I said we're done." Thomasso's tone doesn't rise, but the air in the room shifts—sharp, suffocating. "You keep pushing, I'll start treating you like any other soldier. Is that what you want?"

Leo hesitates, just for a second. Then he backs off and walks out, tension bleeding from every step.

The door clicks shut behind him.

Thomasso exhales once, measured, cold. Then he looks at me.

"Talk."

I nod. "Your son is the rat."

I lay the evidence I hid in my suit jacket upon entering onto my uncle's desk and explain every damning piece. The money trail starts in New York and ends in Leo's offshore bank accounts. I tell him about the shaky alliances Leo's formed down the east coast, and the mercenaries he's recruited that all point to one conclusion: Leo plans to take over our family by force.

We run Chicago for the Sicilian Mafia. Everything west of Lake Michigan to California is ours. At the same time, Matteo Ricci owns the East, from here to New York.

Both families, along with the Russos, La Rosas, and Lombardos, comprise the Commission and answer to the Sicilian boss of bosses, Salvatore Parisi—our *capo di tutti i capi.*

If the Romanos and Riccis keep the peace and the profits flowing, Capo Parisi allows us to run America.

But peace is just a pause between wars.

Because ambition? It never stays buried.

The unspoken truth is that the Romanos and Riccis both want to reign as the sole Sicilian crime family in the States.

And Leo is setting up the board against his own family.

I'm not surprised. He always was a selfish, entitled prick. My aunt Maria, God rest her soul, spoiled him. In contrast, my uncle had no time for a son who despised hard work.

Uncle Thomasso is quiet while he stares at the evidence like a corpse he's debating how to dispose of. The silence stretches, thick with the weight of betrayal. His fingers drum against the edge of his desk in that slow, deliberate rhythm I've learned to dread.

When he finally speaks, his voice is calm—too calm.

"So," he murmurs, eyes still on the files. "The little bastard thinks he's ready to wear my crown."

His hand curls around his glass of gin, and with a quiet crack, it shatters in his grip. Blood trickles from between his fingers, mixing with the liquor. He doesn't even flinch.

"I gave that boy everything," he says, low and cold. "My name. My legacy. A seat at my table. And he dares to build an army behind my back?"

He finally lifts his eyes to mine, and what I see there makes even me stand straighter. Not rage. Not grief. Strategy. Ice-cold calculation edged in steel.

"We won't move on him yet," he says. "No fireworks. No warnings. Let him think he's clever, that he's still in control."

He stands, slowly wiping his bloody hand on a white linen napkin—symbolic as hell, considering the blood will never come out. "I want names. Every coward he's recruited. Every whisper of treason. We won't just cut off the head— we'll gut the whole thing, root and stem."

He pours himself another drink with his uninjured hand and downs it in one swallow.

"He's my son," he says, almost like he's reminding himself. Then his voice drops into something darker. "But if he wants war... we give it to him. Just not on his terms."

I nod, already planning my next move.

Leo started this strike against the family.

But I'm going to end it.

I owe my life to my uncle.

Now, it's time to truly pay my debt to him by terminating his treacherous son.

He can't put a hit out on him or personally kill him because it would make the family look weak. It would appear that the Don cannot control his son or the rats. Acknowledging Leo's scheme would give him more recognition than he deserves.

Leo will die, but it will be carefully orchestrated and not at our hands.

I pull the final piece of information I brought for him from the right inside pocket of my suit jacket and hand it to him.

A photograph of the beautiful woman who's haunted by thoughts since I found out she existed twenty-four hours ago.

The last bastard I kidnapped and tortured for information was Matteo Ricci's trusted valet. He climbed into bed with Leo for a quick payday—and it cost him dearly.

He begged for his life, offering intel that could shift the tide of our cold war with the Riccis. I told him if it were worth something, I'd let him live… just not speak. He already would never walk again due to the crowbar I took to both his knees.

What he gave me? It was worth far more than his tongue.

I point to the photo, my voice calm but deliberate.

"That's Matteo Ricci's daughter."

My uncle scoffs, waving a dismissive hand.

"Impossible. Everyone knows Ricci was made sterile. Capo Parisi ensured it—part of his punishment for what happened to your parents. The man has no heir. His men are fighting like dogs because they know the top seat is up for grabs."

I shake my head slowly and smirk.

"No, Zio. That's what Ricci wants us all to believe. But the truth's more complicated."

I pull up a photo on my phone—Chrisette Asare, mahogany-skinned and radiant, her eyes sharp and captivating even in a still frame.

"This was Chrisette Asare. Ricci's secret lover for years. She gave birth to a daughter twenty-four years ago, named Lucia. The child was kept hidden from the world, tucked away behind a fake name and a quiet life. But Chrisette died last week. Left everything behind—including proof of who Lucia is."

I let that settle before delivering the kill shot.

"Lucia Asare is an accomplished pianist, Ricci's blood, and according to my sources, Leo's next target. He plans to kidnap her and force a marriage."

My uncle's jaw tightens. His hand slams down on the desk, the crystal ashtray jumping.

"That idiota son of mine will get us all killed. Matteo will assume we're behind this. If he harms his daughter, Ricci will take it as an act of war. So will the Commission."

Exactly. That's the point.

"It's what Leo wants," I reply evenly. "A full-on war to cover his power grab. He doesn't just want to run this family. He wants to break it and rebuild it in his image—with Ricci under his thumb."

Thomasso paces once, then stops, breathing hard. His eyes fall back to Lucia's photo. He picks it up and studies it in silence for a long beat.

"She's a beautiful woman," he murmurs. Then he glances at me, a memory flickering in his expression. "A pianist... like your mother. My sainted sister."

I recognize the weight of grief in his gaze. The line he's

drawing between past and future. All he has to do is give the order, and I'll make Leo disappear.

But he doesn't.

Not yet.

Instead, he watches me as I stare at her photo.

I haven't stopped thinking about her since the moment I discovered her.

I had to see her in the flesh. To know if what the valet said was true.

I stalked her from the shadows. I watched her go to her favorite café off Broadway and sip coffee. I followed her to the piano class she teaches at Juilliard. I looked on as she wiped tears after picking up her mother's ashes in the Bronx from a small funeral home, Morris Heights.

I had small cameras planted in her home while she was away.

Just twenty-four hours, and she's already taken up space in my mind like she was carved into it.

Lucia.

Even her name tastes like sin.

Her skin is copper-toned silk, warmed by the sun, but her eyes—God, her eyes—those are Ricci eyes. Cold. Calculating.

But still Beautiful.

She's a walking contradiction. The perfect blend of fire and ice, bred from two bloodlines that were likely never meant to touch.

We Sicilians rarely breed outside of our community. La Familia is diverse and varied, yet still somewhat close-minded.

Another reason why Ricci hid her.

My uncle leans back, his gaze fixed on mine, calculating.

"You know, Rocco, Leo's plan isn't all bad now that I think about it. If he can marry her, so can you. It's time we took our rightful place as the sole family ruling America; we need Ricci to come to heel and accept his new place as second dog. A marriage may be the best way to accomplish that without bloodshed. If Leo had taken her, he would have undoubtedly hurt her. But you, you can keep her."

My jaw clenches. *Marriage was never my plan.*

Getting her in my bed to lick every inch of her until she screams my name? Yes.

Killing that bastard Leo for even thinking of touching her? Yes.

Using our knowledge of her as leverage to bring Ricci to heel? Yes.

But marriage? Hell no.

I'm not built for it. I don't coddle or care, I kill.

I keep women at arm's length. They're unpredictable and manipulative. I fuck them senseless, but never for more than a week or two. I spoil them with lavish gifts while we're together and gently dismiss them when our time is up.

And even if I weren't an asshole with commitment issues, my way would be best. Mafia life isn't conducive to the health and safety of women. Our wars are supposedly fought between men, but women always end up as collateral damage. They carry the deepest wounds of war.

My mother died violently, and she was only loosely affiliated with the family business.

I'm the second most powerful man in the Romano Mafia.

Any woman connected to me will have a bigger target on her back than the Willis Tower.

I don't need that kind of stress in my life. It's enough to focus on keeping my men and myself alive.

My uncle continues, unbothered by my reaction.

"I want Leo to know that I have the same information about Ricci's daughter that he has, but that I'm giving her to you and not him. I'm sure that will rile my idiota of a son up enough, to make him sloppy. He will show his entire hand. Then I will kill him."

I nod, though the weight of everything presses hard on my chest.

I always knew I'd have to marry for the family one day: to build an alliance with one faction or another. But I expected that to be a cold marriage of duty with some girl too naïve ever to make my blood heat.

But Lucia. I haven't even touched her, and I already want to live inside her.

She's dangerous.

"Yes, Don. But..." I pause, meeting his eyes. "Is my marriage to the girl really necessary?"

I already know the answer. In our world, everything of value—power, territory, loyalty—is sealed through marriage or blood. Still, I need to hear him say it.

He doesn't hesitate.

"Yes. You have one week," he says, his voice sharp and final. "Go back to New York, take Lucia. Marry her. Bring Matteo Ricci to his knees."

He turns his back on me, walking toward the bar, but I press again.

"And what if Ricci doesn't care? What if we're wrong about her? What if marrying her doesn't move him at all?"

Thomasso stops mid-pour and glances over his shoulder with a smirk—the kind that's more weapon than expression.

"He hid her, Rocco." He pours the drink slowly, deliberately. "You don't bury what you don't care about."

He turns, glass in hand, eyes gleaming with that deadly certainty I've seen destroy better men.

I nod again, slower this time. There's no turning back.

Lucia Ricci is now the key to winning a war that's just begun.

And she's about to become a Romano.

1

ROCCO

FIVE DAYS LATER

Her image flickers to life —small, fragile, completely unaware.

Lucia Asare.

The Ricci secret. The key. The leverage.

My undoing.

I press two fingers to my lips, eyes fixed on the screen.

She's humming again. Playing the keys softly, lost in whatever world she still believes in.

And I fucking hate it.

I hate that it stirs something in me I thought was long dead.

This should've been simple.

Kidnap. Marry. Control.

Deliver her like a pawn across the chessboard and bend Ricci to his knees.

But I've already broken the rules.

Every night, I find myself right here. Watching. Waiting.

Ruined by a girl who doesn't even know she's started a war.

Leo thinks she's still in play.

He doesn't realize I've already claimed her.

And soon I'll be done watching.

Today, she's seated at her precious piano in a black dress that has ridden up her delicious thighs. Her posture is elegant yet grounded, her fingers gliding effortlessly over the keys as if she were born to create music. The melody is inaudible through the feed, but I don't need to hear it to know it's spellbinding—her touch commands it.

Her long, wavy hair cascades over her shoulders, framing bronze cheekbones and a jawline that speaks of quiet strength. Her full lips press together in concentration, a hint of determination etched in their shape, while her wide, almond-shaped eyes burn with an intensity that hints at visions far beyond the room's confines.

Music is her world, the domain where she reigns. In three days, she's set to make her grand debut at the Lincoln Center's Alice Tully Hall, a performance already drawing the anticipation of critics and admirers worldwide.

Too bad, she'll never make that performance.

Since I left my uncle's office five days ago, I've done nothing but watch her and find out everything about her. I know her mother's medical bills put her in deep debt, and she's drowning. I know that she eats pizza and ice cream every night, only to wake up and run five miles every morning.

I also know that she doesn't sleep.

She's a naughty girl but disciplined.

I've memorized the cadence of her life. The tilt of her head when she's deep in thought. The way her fingers hover over the piano before they strike, like she's giving the keys a warning. Even the curve of her spine when she stretches between rehearsals—I know it all.

It's surveillance. Strategy. Necessary.

That's what I keep telling myself.

But it's a lie.

Because when I watch her, it isn't always for information. It's not just about keeping her safe from Leo's machinations or planning for our eventual confrontation. Sometimes, it's just to see her.

To feel something. To imagine her beneath me, saying my name like it means something.

She's sitting in a barely furnished apartment, and I'm sitting in an office at the top of the Hancock building, furnished in leather, glass, and steel.

Yet, her image rules me.

I'm obsessed.

Then I see the tears. They streak silently down her cheeks, catching in the light, and something in me comes alive. I want to kill the person who caused them, make them suffer for every drop that leaves her beautiful face. At the same time, I want to lick them away, taste her pain, and claim her grief as my own. I want to own every inch of Lucia, down to her tears.

Even more disturbing is the urge to comfort her. I don't do comfort. It's not in my nature. Yet here I am, imagining what it would be like to soothe her, to take her in my arms and make her forget whoever or whatever caused her sorrow.

"Beautiful, isn't she?" Enzo's voice breaks through my thoughts. Standing behind me, his usual smirk softening as he observes the screen.

I ignore the comment, but my jaw tightens. I've seen enough. With a flick of my wrist, I turn off the monitor. "She'll do," I say curtly, masking the unease in my chest.

"She'll do?" Enzo repeats, his voice amused. Turning the monitor back on, he says, "That's one way to put it. But let's keep our eyes on the future, Roc. Now that your cousin knows she's been promised to you and not him, it puts her in more danger."

He looks at her hands fly over the piano like air moves over water with a smirk. "Could it be that you're a bit smitten with your intended because, like your Mother, she's a wonder on the piano?"

If I didn't need him, I'd kill him for knowing me so well.

Enzo Bianchi is the best hacker and security expert on this side of the Mississippi. He should be. Uncle Sam and his band of Naval Intelligence Officers trained him. He's an indispensable pain in my ass and my best friend. Second only to his brother, our resident enforcer, and my capo-Mario.

He's also the father to my goddaughter Aria, so I let him live even when he's being a pain in my ass.

Ignoring his observation, I rise from my chair and glance toward the grand piano in the corner of the room. Its polished surface gleams under the low light, an ever-present reminder of another life—one I left behind long ago. Without thinking, I cross the room and sit on the bench. My fingers hover above the keys before pressing down, coaxing a melody buried deep in my memory. Soft and melancholic notes echo through the room, starkly contrasting the cold calculations consuming my mind.

My mother was a saint. God broke the mold when he made Anna Romano Fieri because all other women were a curse. I've seen what they can do—what they did to my father. His weakness destroyed everything. It's why I stopped playing this piano after they died. Music couldn't protect us. It didn't stop the bloodshed. It's only a reminder of what I lost.

"Still playing that old tune, Roc?" Enzo asks, his tone quieter now. He doesn't need to elaborate; he knows exactly why I'm playing it.

"Chopin's Nocturnes helps me think," I reply, though it's a half-truth. Music is more than a tool; it's a tether to a part of me and my past that I'd rather forget.

The door to my office flies open, and Leo stalks in, entitled as ever. His eyes go straight to the surveillance screens on the wall behind me.

Lucia.

She's still playing through her grief, her fingers now thundering against the keys, her expression determined and glistening from silent tears.

Leo leers. His head tilts slightly as he watches the feed, his mouth twisting into something that makes my blood curdle.

"What's the matter, cousin?" I say coolly, not looking at

him. "Never seen a woman cry without being the reason for it?"

His gaze snaps to me.

"You're wasting time." His tone is clipped, venomous. "While you sit here playing Beethoven, the Riccis are moving into our territory."

I rise slowly from the piano bench, adjusting my cuffs, deliberate in every motion.

"Do you even know who Beethoven is, Leo? Or are you just spitting words you heard in a movie once?"

From the corner, Enzo lets out a sharp laugh and sips his whiskey.

"My money's on Fast & Furious, part six."

Leo's face darkens. His fists curl at his sides.

"Don't patronize me, Roc. I brought our family intel— valuable intel. Ricci's secret daughter is the key to everything. If we're going to use her, we need to act now. I don't know why my father handed this to you. I'm his heir. I should be marrying her. Not you."

Because you're a snake. Venom in your mouth, betrayal in your spine.

I step in, letting the space between us disappear. Close enough to smell the insecurity on his breath.

"Should be," I echo, voice low. "But you're not. Because we both know what happens when you get too close to women, they end up broken... or buried."

He lunges forward, chest puffed, teeth clenched.

"You think you're better than me?"

"No," I say as I casually step back. "I don't think. I know."

His breathing spikes, eyes wide and dark.

"I've been loyal to this family since day one."

Liar.

"And yet," I reply, calm as steel, "you're still not trusted to lead it."

Enzo steps in, hand raised.

"Alright, children. Take off the gloves later. Right now, we've got a mission. Don Thomasso will give the order when the time is right."

Enzo gives me a look. We both know the truth.

The order's already been given. And Leo's not part of it.

Leo looks between us, the tension thick as smoke.

He knows something's off. He smells it. And when his eyes drift back to the surveillance screen—to Lucia—his mouth tightens into a knowing smirk.

He doesn't say a word, but it's all there.

He still plans to take her.

Whether it's through blood, marriage, or force, he's not done.

And that's the problem.

I step between him and the screen, blocking his view. My voice drops to a low threat.

"She's not yours to look at. Not yours to touch. Not yours —period."

Leo sneers but backs off, though his expression leaves no doubt that this isn't over.

There's something in his eyes—a spark of something darker, obsessive. He doesn't just see Lucia as a key to power; he wants her.

The thought makes my blood boil.

"Just remember," he says, his voice dripping with venom,

"if you screw this up, the family will know exactly who to blame, and then she'll be where she belongs."

I wait until the door slams shut behind him before speaking. "He's going to be a problem."

"He's always been a problem," Enzo replies, his voice low. "But this is different, Roc. You saw it too, didn't you? The way he talks about her—it's not just about Ricci or power. He's fixated, Rocco. We've seen this with women he has taken an interest in before. They end up broken dolls,"

I clench my fists, the weight of Enzo's words sinking in.

If he touches her, he'll die.

I glance at the blank screen, and Lucia's vivid image remains. Her life as she knows it is soon to change.

"Fine. We'll take her tonight."

2

LUCIA

My apartment is too quiet.

It always was when Mom worked late shifts for the Lennox Cab Company, but tonight... the silence feels different. Heavier. Like the walls are listening. Like someone—or something-is holding its breath, just out of sight.

I sit at the piano in the living room, my fingers brushing the keys without purpose. A hollow melody stumbles out, broken and incomplete, like my thoughts. In three days, I'm set to debut at the Lincoln Center—a stage I've dreamed of since I was ten. But the weight of it presses down like a stone on my chest.

Maybe it's no surprise. You don't bury your mother and then come back whole.

It's been twelve days since she died, and her absence isn't just a feeling—it's a presence. A shadow curled in every corner. The apartment still smells like her—jasmine and old vinyl—and that makes it worse. The grief is sharp, but the loneliness is sharper.

And now there's this other thing.

This prickling at the back of my neck, like I'm being watched. Like the air isn't mine anymore, I tell myself it's the grief. The pressure. The lack of sleep. However, I still double-check the locks before I play. Still, I keep the blinds half-closed even though it's nearly noon.

The piano used to be my sanctuary. Now, it even feels foreign. The notes don't comfort—they echo. I press down harder on the keys, trying to force something out, but it's like the music doesn't recognize me anymore.

Just like everything else.

Mom would usually hum along from the kitchen while cooking dinner, the scent of simmering Ghanaian spices filling the air—a chale sauce for Cornbeef Stew or a peanut sauce for chicken. Each dish from her homeland always pushed a different sound from her lips. Now, the absence of that comforting noise makes my chest ache.

I lean into the piano, my forehead brushing the cool wood. A framed photo of Mom and me rests on top, its edges worn from years of handling. My fingers linger on the keys as a flash of memory overtakes me.

Mom's laugh is rich and warm, like the songs we'd play together on Sunday mornings. I watch her now, the way sunlight dances on her copper skin as she prepares our breakfast. She's standing at the stove, flipping plantains, her movements unhurried and precise. The air smells sweet and earthy, a comfort I'd give anything to feel again.

"I may not have riches to leave you, my love," she says, low and certain, "but I'll always leave you with the truth."

I look up from the table, surprised by the weight of her words. "The truth about what?" I ask, though I'm not sure I want the answer.

Mom pauses, her spatula hovering over the pan. Her eyes, soft but unwavering, meet mine. "About everything," she says. "About who you are. About love."

"Love?" I laugh, trying to lighten the moment. "What do you know about love?"

She smiles a little sadly and sets the spatula down. "Not much," she admits. "Not the kind of love that lasts, anyway. But that doesn't mean it isn't out there. You have to be open to it, Lucia. Even if it's scary. Even if it doesn't look like you imagined."

A knock at the door startles me out of the memory. My fingers still, the last note hanging dissonantly in the air. I rise, wiping my hands on my jeans as I move cautiously toward the door.

I glance through the peephole. A man stands in the dim hallway, his face partially shadowed. He's wearing a courier's uniform, but what catches my eye is the envelope in his hand—black, with a large, blood-red "R" stamped boldly across the front. Seeing it makes my stomach twist, a chill running down my spine.

"Miss Asare?" he calls, his tone professional but neutral. It's also annoying because he butchered my name. What should sound like "Ah-sah-ree" sounds like "A-say-ree."

I hesitate. I'm not expecting anything. But the man doesn't look threatening, and curiosity nudges me to undo the chain and crack the door open.

"Yes?" I ask, keeping my voice steady. "I'm Ms. Asare."

"This is for you," he says, holding the envelope.

I take it, my fingers brushing against the coarse paper. The envelope's texture is rough and cold against my skin. A faint metallic scent clings to it, sending a ripple of unease through me. Before I can thank him, the man turns and disappears down the hall, his steps echoing faintly.

Closing the door, I return to the piano bench, my hands trembling as I hold the ominous envelope.

My name is scrawled across the front in unfamiliar handwriting. Carefully, I slide a finger under the flap and pull out a single sheet of paper.

The words stop me cold:

> **Lucia,**
> **Your father is Don Matteo Ricci.**
> **He has been watching you from the**
>   **shadows since you were born.**
> **The time for secrecy is over.**
> **Everything you need is enclosed.**
> **Read carefully—your life depends on it.**

My heart hammers as I unfold a second piece of paper. Bank statements. Regular deposits into an account under my name—$10,000 monthly for the past eighteen years. That's over two million dollars, sitting untouched in an account I didn't even know existed. Mom never mentioned money like this, not a man like Matteo Ricci.

The name alone makes my stomach churn.

Not to mention his title. Don-what is this, The Godfather?

Is this note from Mama?

No, this has to be a joke.

My hands tremble as I stare at the documents, fear rising in a swift, uncontrollable wave.

Matteo Ricci.

The name is infamous in New York. He's always in the news—a shadowy figure tied to power plays, criminal enterprises, and a reputation that stretches across continents.

My music professors whisper about the Ricci family like a modern-day legend. They are our most prominent patrons, and here I am, somehow tied to them and tied to *him*?

One thing I know for sure is that Matteo Ricci is very White and very Italian. Me? Though I'm the shade of a butter cookie, I'm Blackity Black, Black-Black, and I always have been.

From my thick, beautiful lips to the generous hips my West African roots afforded me. The idea of being connected to some Italian crime family, let alone being a mafia princess, feels absurd. It doesn't make sense—it can't.

It can't be true. Mom would have told me, wouldn't she?

Perhaps she arranged for this to be sent to me after she was gone. But she wouldn't leave me to deal with this kind of news alone. That wasn't her way. When she was diagnosed with stage three Leukemia, she spent her last twelve months on this earth making sure I knew how to do everything from making meat pies to accessing her death benefits.

Undoubtedly, she would have faced me for something like this.

I reach for my phone, and my first instinct is to call some-one, but who? Mama isn't here to answer. The raw grief I've been holding back since the memorial service surges forward, catching me off guard. Tears spill down my cheeks as I clutch the paper, my breath shallow and ragged.

I'm truly alone.

The sound of glass shattering pierces through my haze, yanking me out of my thoughts. My head snaps toward the kitchen, adrenaline spiking through my veins. The sharp crunch of broken glass under heavy boots follows, each step deliberate and measured.

Someone is in the apartment.

Fear grips me, tightening around my chest like a vise, but instinct kicks in. I shove the documents into my pocket and scramble to my feet, backing away from the piano. My eyes dart frantically around the room. The dim light of the living room casts long, distorted shadows, but one of them moves —a deliberate and menacing silhouette heading straight for me.

"Who's there?" I demand, my voice trembling.

No answer. Just the slow, deliberate sound of footsteps.

I grab the nearest object—a heavy candlestick from the side table—and hold it before me.

"Stay back!" I shout, my voice cracking.

The man steps into the light, and I see the glint of a weapon in his hand. Before I can scream, a second figure emerges behind me, a cloth pressed hard against my mouth and nose. I thrash, the candlestick slipping from my grasp as my vision blurs.

The last thing I see before darkness pulls me under is the

photograph on the piano, Mama's smiling face blurred and fading like a fragile memory slipping through my grasp.

* * *

When I briefly wake, my world is cloaked in darkness. A blindfold presses tightly against my eyes, its rough fabric chafing my skin. The air is cool, carrying a sharp tang of leather and gasoline, mingling with a faint metallic undertone that makes my stomach churn. My wrists are bound behind me, the coarse rope digging into my skin, leaving it raw and throbbing. Every slight movement sends a wave of pain shooting up my arms.

My chest tightens as panic claws its way up my throat. My breathing speeds up, sharp and shallow, as I struggle to piece together what happened. The scent of the vehicle— new leather mixed with lingering cigar smoke—feels overwhelming, almost suffocating. The vibrations of the road hum beneath me, and the occasional car jolt makes my head swim. My muscles scream in protest as I shift, desperate to sit up and orient myself.

"Stay still," a low, unfamiliar voice growls from the front of the vehicle. The menace in his tone chills me to the core.

I freeze, my pulse hammering in my ears. The reality of my situation begins to sink in.

My discovery of Matteo Ricci wasn't a coincidence.

This isn't random.

This was planned.

That's my last conscious thought before I feel a prick behind my ear, and darkness drowns me again.

3

ROCCO

Lucia Asare Ricci is in my home.

Bound and safe in my basement.

I've never slept better.

She doesn't know me—not yet.

But I know enough to unravel her. Enough to manipulate the fragile edges of her identity and twist them until she has no choice but to lean on me for truth.

That's the power of information—and I hold the most explosive piece of all. I know what her father is capable of, and she doesn't.

When I saw the blood-red *R* stamped on the envelope that hit the floor when she was taken, my heart damn near stopped.

I didn't send that note. Which means Leo did.

He found her.

I arrived just in time.

Now she's under my roof, and the game has changed. She might suspect who she is. But she has no idea what that truly means. And I know what her blood is worth down to the penny.

In my world, blood isn't just thicker than water. It's a weapon. A debt. A declaration of war.

Lucia Ricci is no longer an innocent bystander. She's a pawn in a centuries-old vendetta.

Her blood will either soak the floor beneath her or sanctify the sheets of our matrimonial bed.

The choice is hers.

But the victory will be mine.

She's my recompense. My revenge. My reward. And when the time is right, I'll destroy the man who ruined my family... by claiming the one thing he never thought he'd lose.

His daughter.

When my trusted enforcer Mario carried her into the basement, cradled in his arms, I growled in frustration. I sent him to New York to retrieve her; it was too dangerous for me to chance being seen in Ricci's city again so soon.

But he should have called me to the car to retrieve her myself. I may not want a wife, but she's still mine.

No one else—not even Mario—touches what belongs to me from this day forward.

I snatched her from him, staring down at my prize. Her soft skin and shallow breaths stirred something primal. She was utterly at my mercy. From then on, I knew no one else could be trusted near her.

Lucia Ricci will depend on me for everything: food,

safety, information, and—eventually—pleasure. Ours will be the kind of marriage I can tolerate: one I control completely.

One that will keep her safe.

I'm sitting at my desk, watching her through the live feed installed in the basement. The cameras were Enzo's idea—high resolution, night vision, the works. I've never needed a live feed for that part of my house; my basement isn't a prison. It's where I dole out punishments of the pleasurable kind, where women beg for what I can give them.

But with Lucia, I'm undecided. Is she a prisoner or a guest?

From the moment she arrived, I haven't moved from my chair. Watching her quiets the beast raging inside me since my parents were taken from me, and my music was destroyed.

The cameras are so sharp that I can see the pulse at her neck. My fingers tighten on the armrests as I imagine what it would feel like to bite her there.

She stirs and wakes, her expression a whirlwind of emotions: anxiety, terror, and finally, defiance. Her hazel-green eyes dart around the room, assessing her prison. She hasn't touched the water I left for her. She's cautious, strong —a survivor.

Good girl.

Her throat moves as she swallows hard, the effects of Mario's sedative still lingering. My cock tightens at the thought of the nasty bruise she left on Mario's shin for grab-bing her.

She's a fighter.

I should have retrieved her myself. Instead, I had to

watch her struggle on FaceTime. My methods would have been more persuasive. She wouldn't have needed drugs. She would've obeyed—or suffered consequences she'd want to avoid.

She's lucky Leo didn't get to her first. My cousin is a true sociopath, bound by neither reason nor code. If Lucia had fallen into his hands, she'd already be bound in matrimony —and his bed. I kept him busy at his favorite strip club while Mario took care of my beauty.

I'm always one step ahead.

Now that we have Lucia, my uncle Thomasso has sanctioned Leonardo's death. He's done tolerating his madness. Leo's betrayal sealed his fate. There's no mother to beg for mercy, no reprieve—only punishment.

"Roc, the girl is awake. What do you want me to do with her?"

Mario's voice pulls me from my thoughts. I swivel in my chair, narrowing my eyes. How the hell does he know she's awake? Has he been down there?

"You will do *nothing*," I growl. "No one speaks to her or even looks at her without my permission. The basement is off-limits. Got it?"

Mario smirks, amused by my anger. "Possessive much?"

I lunge from my chair, and he raises his hands in mock surrender, laughing. Mario, Enzo, and I have been inseparable since Uncle Thomasso brought me to Chicago from my home in Ravello at sixteen. Mario, specifically, has been more like a brother than an employee. But on this matter, I won't bend.

"She's mine. Is that clear?"

Mario chuckles. "Crystal. You never did like sharing your toys."

Before I can respond, the door swings open without warning, and Uncle Thomasso strides into the room. His presence fills the space instantly.

"Is she awake?" he demands, his voice cutting through the air like a blade.

"She is," I say, sitting up straighter, forcing my tone to remain neutral.

Thomasso's eyes snap to the monitor, narrowing as he takes in Lucia's fragile, disoriented form. He watches her in silence, his expression unreadable. The tension in the room thickens as the seconds drag on. Finally, his lips curl into a thin, disapproving line.

"She looks fragile. You didn't harm her, did you?"

The unspoken accusation lands like a blow. "No," I answer quickly, my voice firm. "She's untouched."

"Good." He doesn't look at me as he speaks, focusing on Lucia. "Because if you mishandle her, you'll ruin everything."

I clench my jaw but hold my tongue. There's no point arguing with Thomasso—not when he's already decided.

He begins to circle the room, his movements deliberate, his hands clasped behind his back. Each step is slow and controlled, carrying the weight of authority. The tension coils tighter with every click of his polished shoes against the floor.

"I've been watching you, Rocco. Watching how you've been watching her."

His words land with a force that makes my shoulders

stiffen. "She's my responsibility," I say evenly. "I'm ensuring she's secure."

He stops in front of the monitor, his gaze fixed on Lucia as if she's a chess piece he's already planned his next ten moves. He's silent for a beat too long before turning his head slightly, his eyes cutting toward me.

"It's more than that," he says, his tone low and dangerous. "I can see it in your eyes. She's already starting to get under your skin."

"That's not true," I snap, sharper than intended.

Thomasso tilts slightly, and the faintest grin pulls at the corner of his mouth—not out of amusement, but a warning. "Lying to me, Rocco, is a mistake. I taught you better."

I give my uncle a tight yes, sir, while Mario tries to contain his laughter.

My uncle doesn't seem to notice anything Mario is doing because his attention is laser-focused on me. "This is why you should fuck more whores Rocco. All you do is work. When I need you on your "A" game, some unconscious woman is already leading you around by your cock. Be careful."

Mario's large 6'5 "frame shakes in amusement. He is a big guy, even bigger than me. My 6'3" frame intimidated everyone when I arrived in the States, but not Mario. My uncle's favorite soldier, Michael "Mickey" Bianchi, and his wife, Beth, adopted him as an infant. They wanted more children, and Beth couldn't have any more after Enzo. They didn't care that Mario was Black.

When I arrived in Chicago, he took me under his wing. He knew what it felt like to be an orphan. He never knew his biological parents, but in his mind, they may as well be dead. No one in the organization gives him shit about his roots because Mickey and Enzo would blow their heads off before my uncle and I burned the body.

Mario is one of the few people not afraid to tell me when I'm full of shit. He knows I'll lay his ass out if he goes too far, so he never does...especially not in front of others. No matter how much I love him, I outrank him. In our world, that shit matters. After a quiet fit of laughter, he gathers himself and walks over to slap me on the back.

"Uncle Thomasso, don't worry. Rocco is the ultimate bachelor. He never stays with any woman long enough for her to come twice, let alone spend the night. So much so that I wondered how he had arrived at the idea of marriage with a woman he barely knew."

My uncle chuckles while helping himself to a glass of whiskey at my bar. "He didn't come up with the idea; I did."

He steps closer, leaning over my desk, his hands pressing into the wood. The room feels smaller under his scrutiny, his presence like a noose tightening around my neck.

"She is the key to bringing Matteo Ricci to his knees," he says, calm but laced with steel. "Nothing more. Don't make the mistake of thinking she's special."

"I won't," I say firmly, my tone clipped.

He studies me for a long, tense moment, his dark eyes probing, searching for cracks in my resolve. I don't flinch. he knocks back the rest of his drink before removing his gaze.

"Good," he finally says, straightening and adjusting the cuff of his tailored jacket. "Because love clouds judgment. And your judgment, Rocco, needs to be flawless."

He turns toward the door but stops halfway, his gaze returning to the monitor. Lucia is rubbing her throat, her face is pale, and her movements are cautious. Thomasso watches her for a beat longer than necessary before speaking again.

"She's pretty; I'll give her that," he says quietly. "But pretty things have a way of becoming dangerous distractions. Don't let her be yours."

Without another word, he strides out, the door swinging shut behind him, leaving the room heavy with his presence.

I lean back in my chair, his warning echoing in my mind —dangerous distractions. Pretty things. My eyes drift back to the monitor, to Lucia's full but fragile frame as she lies back down, her chest rising and falling with shallow breaths.

Mario slouches into the leather couch, shaking his head. "Why her? She's Ricci's daughter. Why not strengthen alliances with a friendly family?"

"Because we don't leave enemies standing," I say simply. "Matteo Ricci cares about her. That makes her valuable. Leonardo saw it, too. He planned to marry her to control Ricci."

Mario exhales sharply, finally grasping the stakes. "And Leo wants to kill Thomasso. He would have undoubtedly used Ricci to do it."

"Exactly," I say. "Leo's ambitions know no bounds. But I beat him to her, and now she's mine."

Mario leans back, his expression grim. "And what will you tell her when you finally meet your soon-to-be wife face to face?"

"Whatever I need to," I reply, grabbing the red Cartier

box from my desk—the pear-cut solitaire gleams in the light. It's perfect, just like her.

Mario shakes his head, smirking. "Good luck, Roc. You'll need it."

I straighten my tie, ignoring him, and head for the door.

Time to meet my bride.

4

LUCIA

*S*omeone is here.

Heavy footsteps echo softly against the stone floor—too deliberate, too sure to belong to anyone but a man.

I can't see him, only the faint silhouette just beyond the reach of a flickering lamp inside this cell. The room is drowned in pitch-black darkness, but the silence around me sharpens every sound, every breath, every shift of air.

I feel him—a subtle disturbance, like a gale building just beneath the surface. The air thickens with energy, coiling down my spine in a slow, aching crawl. He hasn't spoken, hasn't moved closer, but I know he's there. Watching. Waiting.

The floor lamp is to my right. I could reach for it, use it to stand, maybe fight. But I stay frozen. My knees won't cooperate, not when my mind is racing with questions and dread.

Whoever he is, he's the one who sent for me. Who probably sent that note.

His presence looms so large, it feels like the room shrinks to contain it.

Then I smell him.

Sandalwood and smoke, laced with black pepper—earthy, warm, and impossibly male. It doesn't just drift through the air—it claims it.

Where the man who brought me here smelled only like like wealth and tailored suits, this scent offers more.

It's Older. Wilder. More dangerous.

This is what power smells like.

And somehow, I know—without question or logic—that this man is the reason I'm here.

"Bella ragazza, it's time to talk. We have much to discuss."

His voice cuts through the dark—low, rich, and dangerously smooth. The kind of voice that doesn't shout because it never needs to. People probably scramble to obey the moment he speaks.

Every syllable wraps around me like velvet laced with razor wire.

Seductive. Icy. Unmistakably in control.

My heart kicks against my ribs. Fast. Hard. Loud enough, I'm scared he might hear it. I want to see him—need to—but part of me hopes he stays in the shadows just a little longer. Because once I look into the face behind that voice, I won't be able to pretend this is anything less than a nightmare.

I grip the edge of the cot, grounding myself. The lamp to

my right flickers, casting gold along the concrete floor, but it doesn't reach far enough. He stays hidden. Watching me.

Waiting.

In the dark, I feel a little less helpless a little more in control. If he's the kind of man I think he is—and God help me, I *know* he is—he'll feed off any crack in my armor.

I can't let him see the fear clawing at my throat.

Not yet.

Not ever.

I clear my throat, forcing myself to sound steady. "Who are you?" My words hang in the air, clipped and formal, like Mama taught me to do when I needed to command attention. I might be stuck in this cell, but I refuse to let him think he's won.

The sound is scratchy, hoarse—not the pretty, assertive tone I'd perfected over the years, but it's enough to stand on. I cringe inwardly but push forward. "Why am I here? Where are my phone and my belongings? People will be looking for me."

He doesn't answer. Instead, I hear the faint creak of leather as he moves closer, the soft click of his shoes against the concrete. My words don't matter to him; his silence only fuels my unease. The lock rattles, and the heavy door swings open with a metallic groan. He steps inside, closing it behind him with a loud clang that makes me jump.

The lamp clicks to a higher level, and suddenly, *light.*

A brighter beam floods the room. I squeeze my eyes shut against the sting.

When I finally blink them open, I gasp.

He's standing right in front of me.

Towering. Commanding. Unapologetic.

Mafia.

There's something magnetic about him, something that drags the breath from my lungs and coils it into a knot at the base of my throat. I should look away. I *want* to. But I can't.

Olive skin stretched tight over sharp cheekbones. A strong jaw shadowed with just enough stubble to hint at danger. Full lips set in a line that's equal parts arrogance and promise. His black hair is slicked back, not a strand out of place—except for one rebellious curl that's slipped forward, softening a face carved from dominance.

But it's his eyes that shatter me.

Piercing blue. Icy. Electric. Alive with something ancient and unknowable. They don't just look at me—they *see* me. Strip me bare. Peel back the bravado I've been clinging to like a shield and leave me exposed.

Helpless.

And somehow, against all logic and sense, a small part of me doesn't mind.

Because damn it all, why does he have to look like *that*?

I've never been into White guys. There's too much history, expectations, and multiple ways to misunderstand each other. Hell, with my practice and performance schedule, I hardly have time to be into Black guys, either.

But this man? He looks like an orgasm. And he knows it.

I drag my gaze downward, unable to bear the intensity of his stare. My eyes trace the lines of his tailored black suit, from the curve of his broad shoulders to his trim waist. The fabric clings to him, hinting at the strength beneath. He's dressed like a man going to war—a harbinger of death cloaked in elegance. Even his appearance is a weapon.

"Who are you?" I demand again, forcing myself to meet his gaze again. My voice sharpens, edged with the steel Mom always said I needed. "And what could you possibly want with me?"

Slowly, he kneels until we're at eye level. I shuffle back, my thighs chafing against the floor, but his hand lands on my knee, unyielding. Heat floods me at the contact, and I hate myself for the shiver that follows. A whimper escapes before I can stop it. His lips twitch, a hint of satisfaction flickering across his face.

It's been so long since anyone touched me that I don't know how to feel about it.

It takes me a few seconds, but I finally find the appropriate emotion.

But then I do.

Rage.

So, I slap him.

His head snaps back, his eyes blaze, and the icy blue ignites like fire. The muscles in his jaw tighten, and I brace myself for his retaliation. But instead of anger, he seems... amused. Infuriatingly so.

"I am Rocco Fieri," he says, his voice calm but laced with menace. "And you shouldn't have done that, Piccola Ragazza. I had hoped this would be a calm conversation. Now, you will have to be punished."

Both fear and fascination flood through me, but I don't let either show. I lift my chin, defiance pulsing hot in my veins.

"Punished? For what—defending myself against some Gucci-clad gangster with delusions of Godfather grandeur?"

The words slice through the air, sharper than I intended, but I don't flinch.

I *want* to see how far I can push him. I *need* to know what kind of monster I'm dealing with—one who burns hot with rage, or cold with calculation.

For a beat, he doesn't move. Doesn't blink.

Then, his mouth curves—just slightly.

And that's when I realize the most dangerous thing in this room...is how much he enjoyed being challenged.

His grip on my knee tightens, a silent warning. The pressure makes me wince, but I refuse to back down. Neither does he.

He lifts his hand, and I flinch away, prepared for his hit. Instead, he grabs a lock of my hair and rubs the curl between his fingers as he speaks.

The gentle gesture throws me off balance.

"I see the need to explain the rules so that you won't dig yourself into deeper debt with my belt."

His belt. What the hell?

"Rule number one," he says, his tone clipped and cold. "There will be no more cursing. It is disrespectful and unladylike. I will not tolerate it."

I throw my head back and laugh, the sound sharp and bitter. "How would you know anything about being a lady? You're nothing but a monster in a suit."

His hand moves in a blur, wrapping around my neck. The pressure isn't enough to cut off my air, but it reminds me of his strength and control. His thumb brushes against my pulse, and I'm horrified to realize it's racing.

"You think I'm a monster," he murmurs, his gaze locking onto mine. "And perhaps I am. But you'll find I'm not the worst in your orbit."

His rough calluses scrape my delicate skin, contradicting his impeccably dressed and wealthy appearance. I recognize the $2,000 shoes on his feet—lessons from my time working in Neiman Marcus's shoe department aren't wasted.

Hard labor doesn't buy that kind of luxury.

His grip on my neck is a warning, not enough to hurt, but enough to remind me it could change at any moment. When my tears finally spill over, he drags a finger along my cheek, catching one. To my horror, he licks it off his fingertip, his eyes never leaving mine.

Then he leans in, close enough to kiss.

My breath quickens, adrenaline surging through me.

Two thoughts hit like bricks: This man is dangerous, and my panties are soaking wet.

"Lucia," he says softly, his voice like velvet over steel, "you are indeed a *bambina cattiva*, my *palla di fuoco*. But disobedience will not be tolerated—a lesson you'll learn tonight."

He releases my neck, and I cough, sucking in air. The reprieve is short-lived. He clasps both sides of my jaw, forcing my focus onto him.

"You're mine," he states. "You became my possession the moment you were captured and brought here. Everything you thought you knew about your life is irrelevant now. Who you were no longer exists. You'll either accept your place by my side or die—not by my hands, but by the hands of the man who tried to take you first. Your obedience is the only thing keeping that precious Ricci blood flowing through your veins."

What the hell is he talking about? Isn't he the one who took me? Isn't he the one who sent the note? Confusion knots my thoughts, and I decide to play along, for now.

I nod, and he lets go of my jaw.

I fall back, landing on my butt but never breaking eye contact. I'm owed an explanation, and he's prepared to give it. Rising to his feet, he walks to the far corner, hands slipping into his pockets. Quietly, he studies me like a puzzle he can't quite solve.

"You, Lucia Ricci, are the only daughter of Don Matteo Ricci, head of the New York Mafia syndicate."

I snort. "Yeah, tell me something I don't know."

His lips curl into a smirk. "Don't interrupt. I'd hate to add to your punishment."

Punishment?

He steeples his fingers, his glare setting my skin ablaze. "Your father is rich and powerful—my family's natural enemy. He rules New York and the East Coast. We control Chicago and the West Coast. Of course, both families dream of ruling it all."

He tilts his head. "Are you following me, *palla di fuoco*?"

"Yes, I'm following. What is *palla...dee...fuck-oh*? Are you cursing me? You know what? Fuck you! Let me out of here."

Rocco throws his head back and laughs, the sound hoarse and throaty at first, then deep and rich. His entire face transforms, eyes crinkling as he holds his stomach. It's unnerving how gorgeous he looks, how captivating he becomes in that moment. My thighs clench involuntarily.

But he's still a ruthless kidnapper—a common criminal in fancy clothes. My mother may have been foolish enough to sleep with one, but I never will.

The laughter fades, and he focuses on me again. "No, Lucia. I don't let such filth fall from my lips as you do. I would never curse you. *Palla di fuoco* means 'fireball.'"

I roll my eyes. "Oh, so you wouldn't curse me. You'd stalk me, drug me, and drag me to your lair to do God knows what. Maybe rape or kill me. That's not rude at all."

"Enough!" he roars. I press back against the wall but refuse to break eye contact. I won't let this monster see me flinch.

"I don't rape women," he says, his tone cutting. "They come to me willingly. Just as you will one day." He smirks, his gaze flicking over me. "Your mouth, however, seems to do you no favors—unless it's wrapped around my cock. Perhaps I'll help you with that later. For now, *mia palla di fuoco*, you'll listen or face the consequences sooner than planned."

I say nothing, choosing my silence wisely. If I stay quiet, he'll finish his explanation and—hopefully—unchain me. Not to mention, I desperately need to use the bathroom.

Satisfied with my apparent obedience, Rocco nods, then begins to pace in slow, deliberate steps that echo like a countdown. He stops at the edge of the light, just close enough for me to see the wicked curl of his lips.

"My cousin Leonardo intended to take you for himself," he says, voice calm, cruel. "To break you in ways you can't imagine."

A chill skates down my spine, but I lock my body in place. I won't flinch. Won't give him the satisfaction.

"And what about you?" I ask, my voice a whisper sharp as glass. "What will *you* do to me?"

Rocco moves before I can brace myself, closing the space between us like a shadow swallowing light. He leans in, his breath warm against the shell of my ear.

"I will own you," he growls, the promise low and dark. "Mind. Body. Soul. And you will thank me for it."

My breath stutters. His lips graze my jaw—barely a touch, but it brands me. Heat flares under my skin, uninvited, unwelcome. It coils tight in my stomach, tangled with fury, fear, and something far more dangerous.

I *hate* him.

I hate how he speaks.

I hate how he looks at me like he already knows what I'll do next.

I hate how my body reacts—like it's his to command.

"What do you want with me?" I pant, my voice barely audible over the pounding of my heartbeat.

Rocco doesn't answer right away.

He leans in closer, his breath a slow drag against my skin, the scent of power and control curling around me like smoke.

What either of us wants doesn't matter, Piccola. "Because in less than an hour," he murmurs, his voice velvet-drenched in menace, "you'll be my wife."

5

LUCIA

Rocco's promise of matrimony knocks me from my trance, and I shake my head in shock.

"What? I'm not marrying you. I'm not marrying anybody. Are you crazy?"

He glares with disapproval, but his penetrating stare doesn't move me. I need answers.

"Why would your sick cousin, if he even exists, want anything to do with me? He doesn't even know me, yet I'm supposed to believe he had some plot to kidnap and torture me? Why would he do that? WHY THE FUCK AM I HERE?!"

I scream the last question with all the strength my voice can muster, and tears stream uncontrollably down my face. The frustration is unbearable. I'm making a spectacle of myself—something my proud Ghanaian mother taught me never to do.

Chrisette Asare never cowered or created spectacles.

But I'm not as strong as my mother, and I never was.

I'm scared shitless.

Rocco leans back on his haunches to examine me. Yet again, I'm the specimen under his microscope. I feel naked inside and out when he fixes his eyes on me, and I hate it. He's digging out all the parts of myself that I hide away from the world. He ogles them to feed a sick fetish. Refusing to be his meal, I turn away and look at the wall, but he reaches out and draws my face back to him.

"Look at me, Lucia." His voice is quiet and surprisingly tender, like he's coaxing a wild, wounded animal out of a trap. Tethered by fear to his floor, that's exactly how I feel. He strokes an errant strand of my curly hair behind my ear and levels me with his attention.

"You will marry me because that's the only way to save your life and the lives of many others. You will sacrifice your freedom to ensure blood doesn't run down Chicago's streets. I know you don't understand any of that now, but you will as you begin to understand Cosa Nostra and your father's place inside it. You are the key to everything because he who has you has your father in his hand. I can't let Leonardo have that kind of power. You must trust me because life is over as you know it. The life you were living was always temporary. Your debt as Matteo's daughter had to come due at some point. The sooner you accept that, the happier you will be."

A part of me acknowledges his words as truth. Although it defies logic, I realize that my previous way of life has ended regardless of who is to blame. Accepting that makes me tremble with the fear of being caught in a cage constructed by my blood.

To cope, I require a release.

So, I kick him.

The thud echoes in the room, muffled but shocking. He stumbles, and I immediately regret my action. I contract my body to make myself smaller but don't take my eyes off him.

He's eerily calm, and that scares me more than the rage I thought was sure to come. He reaches into his pocket and takes out a key to unlock the cell. I dart my eyes to the door, trying to estimate how far I can go before he catches me, but his eyes arrest me.

I'm not going anywhere.

Wordlessly, he drags me out of the cell. I squirm and pull, trying to escape, but it is in vain.

"Please," I beg, but he only tightens his grip on my elbow as he pulls me behind him.

The rest of what is clearly a basement is still shrouded in darkness, but he navigates the space as if it were daylight. When we reach another door, I'm damn near frantic. He slams open the door and pushes me in. When I enter the small space, a motion light turns on, and I realize it's a restroom.

How did he know?

Relieved to empty my bladder, I get down to business. I know Rocco's standing outside the door, and I wish he'd leave to give me some privacy. But I don't push my luck. I wash my hands and turn the doorknob, but it doesn't budge. I shake the handle several times and realize I'm locked in.

Fuck! He's pissed, and I'm trapped.

The door forcefully opens, and Rocco appears. Except this time, he's discarded his suit jacket and rolled the sleeves of his black dress shirt to his elbows. The ink covering his forearms mesmerizes me. Snaking lines of scripture and symbols curl across his skin, like a story I'll never be allowed to read. His presence is overwhelming, but I steady myself with a deep breath.

He grabs my hand, pulls me out of the restroom, and walks towards the center of the dark room. Then he pauses and looks at me with the intensity of a five-alarm fire.

"You must learn to obey, or you will die in your rebellion. Your demise is not in line with the Romano family plans. So, I'm going to help you learn some discipline."

I'm about to snap back when I pause, a spark of an idea forming. I school my features into something resembling submission and murmur, "I don't understand any of this. You're..." I trail off, pretending to be too overwhelmed to finish.

His eyes narrow slightly, intrigued. "I'm what?" he prompts, stepping closer.

"You're...different from what I thought. Why are you doing all this? Is your cousin, the one you say is after me, as bad as you say?" I ask, keeping my tone soft and curious.

He hesitates, and for a moment, I see something unguarded flicker in his eyes. Regret? Pain?

"He's worse," he says quietly. "I've spent my life cleaning up his messes. I won't let him destroy you, too."

I hold his gaze, sensing this might be my only chance to break through his armor. "Why? What has he done?"

Rocco exhales sharply, running a hand through his hair. For a split second, he looks exhausted, haunted. "Leo doesn't just crave power. He craves suffering. When we were teenagers, he lured a girl from our neighborhood—Caterina

—into his orbit. She was sweet and bright. Too trusting. He impregnated her and then broke her." His voice tightens, his fists clenching. "After she had her baby, I found her barely breathing in an abandoned house. She never spoke again after that. She disappeared. I don't even know if she's alive."

A cold chill spreads through me, but I force myself to stay composed. "And you tried to stop him?"

"I did more than try," he says darkly. "Every time he stepped out of line, I cleaned up after him. Protecting people, he marked. That's why my uncle trusts me. I am the only one who can control him."

"Where's the baby?"

His eyes burn through me. "Enzo adopted Aria-that's her name. He always had a crush on Caterina, but never made a move to claim her. He blamed himself for her death, knowing she would have been his; Leo would not have dared to touch her. Aria is my goddaughter and the center of our entire world. She's four now."

His admission stirs something in me—an understanding, an unsettling attraction to the tortured man before me. Despite everything, there is a code he follows, a line he won't cross—a protector lurking inside the predator.

"Why keep Leo alive?" I challenge.

His lips curl into something between a smirk and a grimace. "Because family is family. And orders are orders, no matter how much I despise him. Plus, it would make the family look weak if we had to take out Don's son for betrayal. He will get his in due time."

Rocco squeezes my hand. "But if he ever touches you, I'll kill him myself."

His words shouldn't comfort me, but they do. And that terrifies me more than anything.

His vulnerability disappears as quickly as it came, but I've seen enough. I hold on to the tiny victory as he grabs my right hand and leads me further into the room. It resembles a swanky lounge with leather couches, low lighting, and a gilded crate in the corner.

A crate? What the hell is this man planning?

He gestures for me to follow, but I hold my ground.

"Lucia! Don't make me ask again." His voice booms, sending a shiver down my spine.

I sigh dramatically, my chin lifted in defiance, and take slow, deliberate steps toward him. If he demands obedience, I'll make him work for it. As I approach, his gaze sweeps over me, lingering on my face, my hair, the curve of my shoulders. His hunger is practically palpable, like a storm building between us.

He sits on the sofa, and part of me wants to run. But I know I wouldn't get far. I'll have to bide my time and play with this madman. His eyes arrest me as he continues.

When I'm close enough, he grabs me by the waist and drops me unceremoniously over his knees. My head hangs precariously close to the floor, and I freeze.

"What the hell are you doing?" I shout, thrashing against his hold.

"Punishing you," he says with a maddening calmness. "You'll thank me later."

6

LUCIA

Once I realize his intentions, I fight like hell. "Let me up, you asshole; what are you doing?"

"Tsk tsk tsk, language, piccolo ragazza. You're making my blood heat, and that's not good for what we have ahead of us. Now, I will bare your bottom and give twenty strikes to your beautiful ass as punishment. Then we are going upstairs to meet my capo, Mario, and a judge to get married. There's no need to argue, as it has already been done. And if you say one more word, I will gag you with your panties while you deal with your punishment."

I thrash wildly, but he places one leg over both of mine, locking me in place—my heart pounds. No one has ever spanked me, ever. Not even my father when I was a child, because the bastard wasn't around. I can't breathe.

"Shhhhh," Rocco leans over, his breath warm against my ear, sending a dangerous shiver down my spine.

"Calm down; you will survive this. Just like you will

survive everything else coming your way now that you are
known as Ricci's hidden principessa, take my hand to your
ass with grace, a punishment you've earned. When it's done,
we can wipe the slate clean, get married, and you can learn
how to wield the power you hold."

If only he knew how powerless I felt.

Nothing about my life was ever by my design. My mother
planned my musical career. And now, I'm being forced to
marry a monster. I suck in a deep breath, trying to steady my
thoughts.

"And if I refuse?"

I feel Rocco shrug. "Then I will let you go, and you can
deal with Leonardo and his hounds alone. I promise you
won't last twelve hours. He knows you're missing by now,
which will only intensify his search. Your father has no idea
what's happening or that you even know who he is. I hate
him for a myriad of reasons and would prefer to kill him. But
I have to push all that aside and do things I don't like to
protect our family; that includes keeping you alive. Matteo
can't protect you from Leo, and even if he could, would he?
The man hasn't contacted you in twenty-four years."

His words hurt, tearing open an old wound I've kept
buried. Longing. Rejection. I longed for a father, but he never
came. He never searched for me. My mother never discussed
him, and I assumed the worst. But that didn't stop me from
wanting him. Every little girl wants her daddy. I was no
different. The tears that fall now are no longer out of fear—I
hate Rocco Fieri for making me feel this way. I also fear him
because he's my father's enemy.

How can I trust that he'll keep me—his enemy's only daughter—safe?

I whimper as he strokes my ass gently, his touch igniting something I refuse to acknowledge. My body betrays me, my breath catching as warmth spreads through my core. Though harsh, his voice wraps around me like a possessive embrace.

"I can take care of you, Lucia, but only if you obey me. I will not tolerate insubordination or reckless behavior. You must learn to control your emotions, or this life will eat you alive."

Would he let me go? Do I even want to test that theory? A part of me already knows the answer.

I don't tell him about the note that arrived at my home before he and his goons arrived.

I don't tell him that I've felt eyes on me since my mother died. Was it Leo? Or Rocco?

I don't know why, but I trust Rocco isn't trying to hurt me. He's dangerous, but not in the way Leo sounds. I can sense it. Eventually, I will escape him, married or not. But for now, I need his protection.

Resigned to what's coming, I take a slow, deep breath and whisper, "I'll stay."

Rocco's hand presses against my back, stroking me in slow, measured movements. The rhythmic motion is hypnotic, lulling me into a trance. I don't know how long he has been doing this, and within moments, my body betrays me again, melting into his touch. My eyes flutter shut, my mind slipping into a haze of warmth and exhaustion.

Then it stops.

His hands are gone, and a sharp chill rushes over my skin in their absence.

"Lucia, it's time."

With no preamble, he flings my dress up, baring my black thong. A low growl rumbles from his chest, vibrating through my bones, and I fear being utterly devoured for a brief moment.

His hands roam my curves, tracing slow, deliberate circles over my ass. The sensation is maddening, each touch igniting sparks under my skin. It starts gently—almost soothingly—before shifting into something darker, more demanding. A delicious pressure kneads into my flesh, sending waves of heat curling through my belly.

I'm dripping wet.

What the hell is wrong with me?

The first smack lands with a sharp, stinging snap, and an unbidden moan spills from my lips.

Do I like this?

No, I'm just horny. That must be it.

I haven't had sex in three years. No time, no interest. Men come with complications and expectations. My Lelo Enigma vibrator never demanded my submission, never teased me to the brink of pleasure to deny me release.

Maybe my lack of sex with an actual man has ruined me.

The third smack sends me rocking forward, my core pulsing with need.

If he keeps this up, I swear I'll come like this.

The fourth, fifth, and sixth slaps come rapidly, each strike igniting something dangerous in my bloodstream. The pain and pleasure mix into a potent elixir, and my mind starts to float, weightless in the haze of sensation.

Fuck... I'm going to come...

Just a little more... just a few more...

But then he stops.

I let out a strangled whimper, my body trembling in protest.

He chuckles darkly, his fingers pressing possessively into my hips. "So, my little palla di fuoco likes having her ass played with. Too bad I won't let you come. Bad girls don't get orgasms until they've atoned for their sins. That was only a warm-up. Now, your real punishment begins."

I whimper, trying to grind my clit against his thigh, desperate for friction, but he holds me in place. His grip tightens, his hand sliding up to clasp my neck. The silent message is clear: he's in control.

I struggle, thrashing against him, but my energy burns out too quickly. Defeated, I let the tension drain from my body, surrendering to him completely.

Rocco shifts his grip, his fingers threading into my hair. My tears fall freely now, but they're no longer just about fear. They're about everything I've lost and never had, and the terrifying reality of what's to come.

He leans in, his breath hot against my ear, his voice a dark promise. "Now, mia palla di fuoco, tell me why you're being punished."

7

ROCCO

Growing up, Lucia probably never envisioned her wedding day like this. But then again, I doubt she ever imagined a man like me would be the one standing across from her, waiting for her surrender.

She likely imagined worldwide debuts as a classical pianist.

She craved standing ovations and awards, not parties celebrating the ultimate prize of a man's name.

My name.

I imagine there were no fantasies of white dresses or Rolls-Royce Phantoms delivering her to lifelong purgatory. Her career and independence meant too much to her to get caught up in the fairytale of matrimonial bliss.

Still, you can't be a woman in America without the wedding machine being jammed down your throat. Thanks to cable television, she knows what a wedding is supposed to look like. However, nothing on TLC or Bravo could prepare her for this moment.

Lucia stands beautifully in my office, trying to ignore her sore behind, wearing the same filthy dress in which she was kidnapped. She's also nursing a growling stomach. I hear the evidence as I hold tightly to her wrist. She's reached behind her and snuck no less than five mints from my desk since we've been here.

She's trembling, not with fear, but with fury. I admire it, truly. She holds her head high despite knowing there's no way out. She's magnificent in her defiance—an inferno refusing to be extinguished. And God help me, I crave her submission just as much as I desire that fire.

The priest clears his throat. I prefer to use a judge in a situation like this. And that was my plan, until the judge I hired was found slaughtered in his chambers an hour ago.

Leo.

"Shall we begin?" He presses.

Lucia doesn't even look at him. Her gaze is locked onto mine, those deep brown eyes seething with hatred. She speaks before I can, her voice steady.

"I won't do this."

A slow smirk tugs at my lips. "Oh, but you will."

"I'd rather die."

I step closer, closing the space between us, my grip tightening around her wrist. "Dramatic, la mia piccola palla di fuoco. But we both know you don't mean that."

She jerks, trying to free her arm, but I don't budge. And then I see it. The flicker of something calculating in her eyes. She's planning something.

I let her believe I don't notice as she subtly shifts, her fingers inching toward her sleeve. It's almost admirable, her desperation. The way she's willing to grasp at any possibility of escape, even when the odds are stacked against her.

Then, in a flash, she moves, fingers closing around a hidden ice pick. My little warrior. Clumsy but brave.

She lunges, aiming straight for my throat, but she's predictable. Before the blade can touch me, I catch her wrist in midair, twisting just enough to send the weapon clattering to the floor. Her sharp cry of pain barely registers.

The priest steps forward, ready to intervene, but I lift a hand.

"No," I say, keeping my voice calm. "Let her have her fight."

Her chest rises and falls with each ragged breath. She's panting, her entire body rigid with anger, but I see that flicker of regret behind her bravado.

I grip her chin, forcing her to meet my gaze. "That was a mistake, Lucia."

"Go to hell," she spits.

I chuckle, stroking my thumb over her jaw. "Oh, Lucia. You are going to learn, my love. You will fight, you will rage, but in the end? You will submit."

She shudders, and for a split second, I wonder if fear courses through her-or something else.

The priest, looking increasingly uncomfortable, clears his throat again.

"Priest, leave us," I command him. "Wait outside the door. It seems my Piccola Ragazza needs a reminder of why we're here."

Lucia gasps and pulls against my grasp. "Hold on," she shouts. "I thought you said we were coming upstairs to meet a judge. Do you mean to tell me you dragged an actual man of the cloth into this blasphemous sham of a wedding?"

Looking uncomfortable, the priest quickly exits the room, and Mario comes out of the shadows and steps closer to Lucia and me. From the surprised look on her face, she must not have realized he was in the room.

I turn back to Lucia, my hand still firm on her arm, anchoring her in place. "Now, about your inquiry."

She stiffens as I tilt her chin, forcing her to meet my gaze. "Judge Robertson was supposed to be here tonight, but plans changed."

Mario clears his throat, stepping forward. "Roc, do you think this is wise?"

His voice cuts through the air, triggering something in Lucia. Her entire body stiffens, and her breath hitches. I see the realization dawn on her face—the recognition.

Mario. He was the one who took her from her home, the one who shoved her into the car and brought her here.

Her eyes snap to him, wide and filled with something darker than anger. Something close to terror.

He would never harm her. But it's not in my interest for her to know that right now.

Mario glances at me but doesn't step back. "The more she knows, the bigger a target she becomes."

I exhale sharply, ignoring his concern. "She's already a target, Mario."

I pull my phone from my pocket, flipping the screen

toward her. The image of the judge, carved up and left in his blood, makes her visibly pale.

But still, she looks at the photo closer and then huffs in shock. "Is that an LR carved into his chest?"

I nod. "Yes, Piccola Ragazza, Leo Romano killed him before he could serve us this evening. So, I called our family priest."

Lucia stares at the mutilation, realization dawning behind her horrified expression. She finally understands what she's running from, what I'm protecting her from.

Her breathing grows shallow, panic threatening to take over.

"He's going to kill me," she croaks.

I grip her tighter, my voice dropping. "No. Breathe, little one. You're safe."

She swallows hard, her hands trembling. But when she looks up at me, there's something else in her eyes.

It's not trust.

It's need. Dependence. Fear.

Good. She's learning.

* * *

A few moments and two shots of whiskey later, the priest returns to his spot in front of my desk.

Lucia is more relaxed, and I'm getting impatient.

"Let's get this over with," I say, turning back to him.

The vows are simple and move quickly. I say I do, but unsurprisingly, Lucia refuses to. Her fear doesn't force her into compliance.

"I don't consent to this," Lucia hisses under her breath.

"You can force me to stand here, but you can't make me agree."

I'm impressed. But this is not the time to admire her strength.

I sigh, shaking my head. "Lucia, I was hoping you'd show some grace now that you know what's at stake. But you insist on making this difficult." My voice drops, smooth and hypnotic. "Very well. We'll do it the hard way."

She doesn't see it coming.

With a swift motion, I pull her flush against me, my hand wrapping around the nape of her neck. Her breath hitches, her body going still. I lean in and grind my hard dick against her center, my lips brushing her ear.

"Say it," I command, my voice low and firm.

She shakes her head, her nails digging into my chest.

I trail my fingers down her spine, slow and deliberate. "You are mine now, Lucia. Whether you fight or not."

Her body betrays her, arching slightly at my touch before she catches herself. I sense her hatred, but I also feel her confusion, her body at odds with her mind.

I pull back slightly to look into her eyes. "Say it, Lucia. Or I will put a call through to Leo and tell him exactly where you are."

Her breath stops.

For the first time, genuine fear flickers across her features.

"You wouldn't," she whispers, her voice breaking slightly.

I smile, but it isn't kind. "Try me."

She knows I won't let him have her. But she also knows I

will make her believe I would. That's all I need. Her fight isn't worth her life, not when she's smart enough to know better.

Her lips tremble, her fingers clenching into fists.

"I..." She swallows hard. Her pride is thick in her throat, choking her.

I press a hand against the small of her back, keeping her close. "Say it, Lucia."

She exhales sharply, hatred burning in her gaze. "I do."

The priest rushes through the rest of the rites, sensing the volatility in the air. And when it's done, I tilt her chin up, claiming her gaze before I claim her mouth.

"There," I murmur. "That wasn't so hard, was it?"

Then I take her mouth, firm, deliberate, mine.

Not a kiss. A claim. A warning. A promise.

Her lips tremble against mine, soft and defiant, but I don't give her space to think, to breathe, to pull away. When she finally yields, I devour her like she's already mine—because she is.

This isn't tender. This is possession.

I kiss her like I own her body, her breath, her future.

And when she gasps, I swallow it whole—the sound, the surrender, the last bit of air she has left.

She'll remember this.

She'll remember *me*.

Because from this moment on, there is no going back.

She is mine now.

And I will break her beautifully.

8

LUCIA

I t only took five minutes to become Lucia Asare Fieri.

Surprisingly, that fact washes away a modicum of the uncertainties and regrets I've been collecting since my mother was diagnosed with terminal cancer.

For the past year, I've been adrift in a world that no longer makes sense. Not even my music brought me the feeling of rightness it used to.

The note about my father only deepened my confusion, unraveling what little stability I had left. And now, in a twist of fate I never saw coming, I belong to a man I barely know— one who radiates danger and dominance in equal measure.

Now he owns me. Legally, I am his... just as he is mine.

A shiver rolls through me, but I don't know if it's dread or something far more dangerous—something dark and needy that coils in the pit of my stomach.

Rocco's grip is firm but not harsh as he leads me upstairs, his presence towering beside me. The weight of the massive pear-shaped diamond set in platinum on my left hand feels suffocating—a perfect noose around my neck. And yet, I can't deny the way it gleams under the chandelier, a symbol of the power he now wields over me.

I love it.

I hate it.

I crave it.

He pauses when we reach the massive oak door at the end of the hall. His smoldering gaze locks onto mine as he extends a hand, a slow, deliberate invitation.

"After you, Mrs. Fieri."

My stomach clenches at how he purrs my new name, his voice dripping with possession. My nipples tighten, my thighs press together, and I know—deep in my bones—that this man will ruin me.

I know it.

A slow smirk curves his lips, like he knows exactly what I'm thinking.

"It's time to feed you, Lucia."

The words send heat slamming between my legs because I know he's not just talking about food. His meaning is layered, thick with promise. My stomach twists at the real-ization that my plans for a marriage in name only are already obsolete. I was a fool to think I could keep Rocco or "Roc," as Mario called him, at a distance. He's too perceptive, too relentless. He knows my body wants him. He's felt my shivers and heard my ragged breaths, and now he intends to claim everything I've been so desperately trying to hide.

I swallow hard, my pulse thrumming in my ears. I tell myself to turn around, to set boundaries, to fight. But my traitorous feet move forward, stepping into the darkened room that will seal my fate.

The heavy door swings shut behind me, reverberating through my bones. I barely have a moment to process before Rocco's mouth crashes onto mine, his lips demanding, his tongue sweeping in and stealing my breath. He consumes me, devours me, makes me forget my own damn name as he pins me against the door. My fingers claw at his shirt, my body arching against his like it belongs there.

A needy whimper escapes me when he fists the fabric of my filthy dress and rips it down the middle, the remnants of my past shredded in his hands.

I gasp, my hands instinctively flying to cover myself, but he's faster. Rocco catches my wrists in one firm grip and presses them above my head, pinning me completely. My exposed skin burns under his gaze, my breath shallow as I watch the hunger darken his features.

"Don't hide from me, Lucia," he murmurs, his free hand skimming down my ribs, tracing the curve of my waist. "I won't allow it."

I don't recognize the sounds leaving my mouth, the way my body trembles in his arms. I should be fighting him. I should be afraid.

Instead, I feel like I'm falling down a dark, delicious hole.

Rocco watches me unravel, his grip tightening, his breath warm against my ear. "You're mine now, little one. And I intend to teach you exactly what that means."

I'm so fucked.

9

ROCCO

I strip her clothing away until she's left in her lace panties.

Stepping away, my body holds a hunger it won't contain. Lucia's delicate hands cover her breasts, but I snatch them away.

"Don't hide from your husband. Your body is my reward, Lucia. Do you understand?"

Her fists ball up at her sides, but she nods. She's upset and embarrassed, but her pointy nipples reveal she's also horny. I relish the vision as I step closer and run my hand down the side of one breast and the other. She shudders, and I smirk.

"Besides piccola ragazza, you are beautiful, and your body is irresistible. These are weapons that, when used properly, are as lethal as an AR-15."

She huffs. "I won't lease my body out to win favors or fights. Did you marry me to be your whore? I won't allow you to reduce my life to a bargaining chip you pass out to win wars."

The crack in her voice reveals her true feelings. She really must learn to hide her emotions. She's scared and timid as a dove. My dove.

I wrap my hands around her neck and hiss. "You're not my whore; you're my wife, la mia piccola palla di fuoco. But that doesn't change that men are stupid beasts rendered senseless and numb when their dicks get hard. That, my love, is a biological fact. Be proud of what these sweet tits and that pussy of yours can do to a fool. Walk boldly in your power."

I reach down and yank her lace panties against her pussy until they tear. Her moans awaken the beast in me, and I place a kiss behind her ear.

"Until I tell you otherwise, you are to remain naked. Am I clear?"

She gulps and nods. I release her neck and lead her by the hand to the bathroom.

"Come," I growl.

My fingers tighten around hers. I can't trust Lucia to stay without the shackles of my grip. She'll run because she doesn't trust me not to kill her in cold blood, or worse, take something from her she doesn't freely give. She'll learn that I take care of my possessions.

I will never harm her. I won't enjoy this sweet body of hers until she gives it to me. I don't rape women, and I don't tolerate men that do. Their lives end by castration before I feed their balls to them. They choke to death on their filthy blood.

However, that doesn't mean I won't push her comfort limits. Or that I won't punish that beautiful ass of hers if needed. Her safety is paramount, and security requires her obedience. I may demand she stay naked and talk dirty until I make her blush. But that's only to prepare Lucia for her new reality as a mafia princess.

One day soon, she may have to stare down the end of a gun barrel or be kidnapped by our enemies. She can't allow her nakedness and some misplaced sense of modesty to break her before the fight begins. My mother died with dignity and defiance. Lucia must own and love every inch of herself with reckless abandon. It's clear she doesn't know how, but I will teach her.

I also won't lie to her. Whether she allows me to fuck her tonight or next week without the proverbial bloody sheets, our union is vulnerable. She may or may not be a virgin. Either way, I can tell her experience is limited.

A woman who's accomplished as much as she has in the classical music world has little time for passionate affairs, and the barriers around her heart are as tall as the fucking Berlin wall was in the eighties. My fireball isn't a fan of vulnerability; that much is clear.

I step into the white-marbled Roman shower and turn on all four jets. The water comes like a waterfall, and steam rises immediately. My clothes are soaked, but I don't care, especially when I see my new wife eyeing my chest through the wet fabric.

I take care of myself and never miss a day of training at the gym. Between weightlifting and Krav Maga sessions, my body is well-defined, muscular, and lean.

"Do you like what you see, Lucia?"

Her eyes immediately switch from fire to ice. I smirk. "You should close that mouth of yours before I think it's an open invitation to place something in it."

I allow her to snatch her hand from my grasp so I can strip. Unbuttoning my shirt, I eye-fuck her the entire time. She's probably wet right now.

"You're such an asshole, Fieri. I was staring because I wondered how a monster like you could have such a pretty shell to hide beneath. What unsuspecting youth's blood do you drink to pull it off?" She tilts her head to the side. "I mean, how old are you anyway, fifty?"

I laugh, but continue to undress. My wife is feisty. Her tone is full of vinegar, but her eyes still beg me to make her come. If she thinks her defiance will stop me from pulling my dick out, she's wrong. We are getting in this shower together so I can tend to her properly. She's had a rough twenty-four hours, and I haven't shown her anything but dominance and death. It is time to adjust her opinion of me, and it starts by bathing my fascinating new wife. Lucia needs to relax.

Stepping under the spray, I hold my hand out for her to join me. She crosses her arms over her chest and scoffs, but I stand erect and wait. She will come, and I won't force her. After a moment, I speak.

"Lucia. Join me. I know you must want a shower by this point."

After I wipe away the water running down my face, I catch her scowl. "I do want to get clean, but not with you. I'd rather shower alone."

"That's too bad, la piccola ragazza. You haven't eaten in

over a day, and you're already a little wobbly on your feet. I'm not trusting you in this shower alone. It will be my pleasure to bathe you and take care of that beautiful body of yours."

"I'm not a child." She tuts. "I can wash myself."

I step from under the spray, praying God grants me the patience he knows I've never had. I've never worked so hard for a person's obedience. At first, it was cute; now, I find it exasperating.

"Yes, Lucia, I know how old you are, even if you aren't familiar with my age." I'm thirty-seven. Thank you very much. "You can wash yourself, but why do that when I am here to do it for you? You've had a horrible time with me, and it's time for some pampering. Come, you've already married me, so you may as well enjoy the perks."

After a beat, she releases a heavy sigh and walks into the shower directly under the spray. I smile to myself over the minor victory.

Stopping behind her, I watch as she runs her hands through her hair while letting the water cascade down her face. She's exquisite. My dick is hard and long as a battering ram, but I keep my control. Leaning down, I squirt some Dior Homme body wash into my hands and run them over her neck and shoulders. She will smell like me until we can get her some things of her own, but I don't mind. I rather like it.

Taking my time, I massage the soap into her tense muscles. I rub hard until I feel her relax under my touch, and when I hear a faint moan, I know I've hit pay dirt. She needs this. Now, I only want to listen to her make that sound again. I want to make her whimper and moan until she's nothing but a pile of needy goo in my capable hands. I continue my ministrations down her body and allow the spray to rinse off the soap I've applied.

She freezes and shrieks when I grab my shampoo and squeeze a dollop into her hair.

"What is that?"

Confused, I shrug. "It's only shampoo, Lucia. What's the matter?"

She turns to face me and sighs wearily.

"Fieri," she bites.

I hate when she calls me by my last name. Every syllable places a distance between us, but I will fix that soon.

"I know you think you planned this forced marriage down to every minute detail, but did you stop and think about the heritage of your wife? Supposedly, I'm half-Italian, but I'm Ghanaian. You can't just put any old shampoo into my hair unless you want me to end up with a dried-out, brittle bird's nest on my head. I need a co-wash and lots of leave-in conditioner to tame this mane."

She points at the wavy dark curls spilling down her back and takes a deep breath. I regret not anticipating her needs, but this will be the last time that happens.

"You think I didn't notice you're an African Goddess?" I step closer, pulling her back from underneath the spray and into my arms. "I'm mesmerized by your warm-toned skin. It resembles mine but has a sweet toasted almond undertone instead of olive."

Nuzzling her hair, I breathe her in. "Your hair is thick and wavy like my mother's." When I run my hands through the curly strands, they lengthen down her back. "Only with tighter curls and definition."

I press my thumb against her lips, and my eyes beg them to open for me. She does, and I slip my thumb inside. To my delight, she swirls her tongue around it and sucks me as I slide it out. A groan escapes the back of my throat, but I keep my composure.

"These lips are thick and plump, like the Yoruba art I've obsessed over in galleries for years. So yes, beautiful, I notice and admire your African roots. I just didn't know that meant you needed a different shampoo."

Against her wishes, she smiles at me, and I feel like I've won the fucking lottery. That smile needs to come to the surface more often.

"It's okay," she whispers. "You didn't know." Leaning behind me, she picks up my conditioner and reads the label. "I guess we can use this until I get some of my things."

I nod and turn her back toward me once more. I squeeze a generous amount of conditioner in my hands and massage it on her scalp. She melts and relaxes her head against my shoulder while my mouth gets busy, stealing kisses all along the side of her jaw. When I've rinsed the last of the conditioner out and feel her hair is sufficiently clean, I turn her around and thank my lucky stars as her lips melt into mine.

When we come up for air, I stroke her cheek. "Let me make you come, piccola. I want to make you feel good and watch you fall apart . I know you need it."

She breathes heavily and looks at my chest. I place a finger under her chin so she will look up at me, but she shakes her head and looks down again. "I don't... I can't...."

Her protests are half-hearted. She's nervous, not adverse. I tip her chin up to level her eyes on me again. "Are you innocent? Lucia? Tell me the truth and tell me now. Virginity is nothing to be ashamed of."

She blows a breath and closes her eyes, but I pinch her hip with my free hand, and she puts her eyes back where they belong, on her husband. Anger flashes in her gaze.

"I've had sex before." Her bravado grows, and she shakes her head. "I'm a grown woman, Fieri. You think I've never taken a dick before?!"

I wish I hadn't asked. Now all I want to do is hunt down every bastard that ever got the privilege of seeing her naked and claw their fucking eyes out before I kill them slowly, but I remain calm.

"How many lovers have you had, and when was your last one?"

Her eyes widen in shock, and I pull her from under the water spray.

"That's none of your business!" She hisses.

"Ahh, but that's where you're wrong, piccola. It is my business, and I need to know how much that sweet cunt of yours can take because I will take it one day soon. You will beg me to; our precarious situation will call for it. There's no shame in your sexual history. Just tell me so I can take care of you."

She shakes her head, and her eyes plead with me. "I'm not ready to have sex with you yet. It's too much and too soon."

Her honest admission tells me everything I need to know. She hasn't slept with many men because sex means something to her, but the sadistic side of me wants her to confess the number in her own words. I love her discomfort. It makes her vulnerable, and that's sexy as hell.

I nod. "Noted. Now tell me. How many lovers and when?"

"One, okay!' She yells. "Are you happy now? One! And it's pathetic. He was my boyfriend freshman year in college, so it's been about five years since I've had sex."

The beastly part of me is delighted. I'm sure that person did not know what they were doing at that age. I swiftly lift Lucia by her waist and press her against the shower wall.

"Yes, Lucia. I'm happy, and now I will make you come so hard you forget your fucking name and his. It will only require my tongue and fingers. Are you ready?"

She sucks in a breath and gives a slight nod. That's all I need.

"Good girl."

I drop to my knees and open her legs before lifting her body. "Place your legs on my shoulders."

She obeys, and I press her thighs open as wide as possible to hold her in place. Then I dive into my feast like a starving man possessed.

I lick her pretty little clit with enough pressure to make her drip on my tongue. She wants to push her pussy into my face and set the pace, but she can't at this angle. Right now, she's mine to control and tongue fuck anyway I want.

I feel her back arch against the wall as she clutches the back of my head with one hand and braces herself against the wall with the other.

"Oh, fuck!" She cries out, and I chuckle against her wet and open pussy.

I continue to lick from the crack of her ass through the wet seam of her pussy and back again while she shakes and grabs my hair. Once I know she's on the precipice, I remove my head, and she whimpers. I throw her a wicked gleam when I give her pussy two hard slaps and press my two middle fingers inside her to pump slowly.

"Oh, Fieri... please... please.."

I chuckle. "Do you need to come, piccola ragazza? Do my fingers feel good inside this tight, wet pussy? Should I make you gush down my arms?"

I press my thumb against her clit and apply pressure. She jerks and makes a low bleating noise.

"Please..." she whines.

"Ask me nicely, Lucia. Call me Roc. Beg your husband to make you come."

My thumb moves in soft circles over her clit, and I add a third finger inside her.

"Oh FUCK, Roc," she screams. "Please make me come, Roc, please."

"With pleasure, Lucia." I remove my thumb and continue to pump vigorously inside her and place my lips on her swollen little clit to suck it for all its worth. She immediately blesses me with a gush of sweet cream and moans like a wounded animal as she slaps her hand against the shower tile in desperation. Her body shakes and trembles, but I keep kissing her sweet pussy to make her ride the orgasm until there's not one sensation left.

When she finally stops convulsing and comes down from her high, I remove her legs from my shoulders and stand up.

She slides down the shower wall, but I catch her and carry her over to the shower bench.

"Wait right here, wife."

She does as I ask and watches me return under the spray to wash my body. I take my time and soap up my entire form, giving her the show of her life. When I get to my hard cock; I pump it vigorously. I grunt as I call her name while my wasted seed spills over the shower floor. One day soon, it will be deep inside her.

Lucia's eyes dilate, and I know I can have her for a fucking dime right now, but it's not time. She needs food and rest.

I rinse off and then pick her back up in my arms. She's silent when I bring us out of the shower, and she doesn't say a word while I towel dry her hair and body. Lucia makes no sound when she takes the towel and returns the favor. Her touch makes me hard as a fucking rock again, but if she notices, she doesn't let on.

Turning away from her, I walk to the bathroom closet and pull out two fluffy, warmed-up robes. I place one on Lucia, who yawns as I tie her sash. She's exhausted. Then, I quickly place mine around my body. I take her hand and lead her to the bed, where a silver tray with food awaits us.

A small smile breaks across Lucia's face as her stomach grumbles.

"What's all this?"

I chuckle, opening all the domes to reveal every dinner food imaginable. There's pasta, steak, chicken, steamed vegetables, mashed potatoes, rolls, and cheesecake. Lucia picks up one roll and starts nibbling, and she moans when she bites into the buttery bread.

"If you keep making noises like that, I'm going to rip that robe off you and eat your sweet pussy again for dinner."

Lucia blushes. "Please don't. I don't think I can have another orgasm like that. I've never come so hard in my life."

She will have many.

I nod. "Good, that's how I want you always to feel." I walk over to her and lift her onto the bed. Then I open her legs and kneel on the floor between them. She observes me as I take a spoonful of potatoes on a fork and bring them to her mouth. "Here, let me feed you."

She swallows her bread. "Roc, that's unnecessary. I can..."

I cut her off with a wave of my other hand. "If you tell me you can do something yourself again, I will put you over my knee and tan your hide. We've been through this. You can do many things, but why should you if I'm here to serve you? Now come. Open your mouth for me, piccola ragazza."

She obeys, and I place the fork in her mouth. As I slide it out of her mouth, her tongue licks the salty potatoes off the fork. It's the sexiest thing I've ever seen. As I fix my lips to tell her so, I hear a loud "Boom," and the food rattles to the floor. The building shakes as two more thunderous booms crash against it.

Fuck! He's here.

My enemy is trying to breach the doors.

Lucia screams and falls into my arms as I curse the universe.

I wanted at least one night of peace to prepare my wife for what was coming. But there's no putting this war off any longer. I

I hope Lucia's ready.

10

LUCIA

Rocco's arms clamp around me like a vise as we crash to the ground. The breath is slammed from my lungs. My back hits cold marble, his weight shielding mine. We don't just fall—we're pulled into a different world. One where sanity doesn't exist and fear is the only thing that breathes.

I can't think.

I can't move.

My mind detaches, floats somewhere above me, watching this horror unfold as if it's happening to someone else. I pray—hard and fast—that I'll black out. That unconsciousness will spare me from what's coming.

But Rocco won't let me escape.

His hand clamps over my mouth, silencing me. His piercing blue eyes lock onto mine, sharp enough to slice through my panic. I thrash, trying to twist away, but I'm pinned. Then, another pop—gunfire closer this time—and tears spill down my cheeks in hot, terrified streaks.

His expression softens. Only slightly. But enough to make the storm inside me stutter.

Then the bullets tear through the bedroom door.

I nearly pass out.

This is it. I'm going to die.

How poetic. I'll die in a stranger's bed, married to a man I barely know—because my mother once fucked a mafia don. That's the sum of my life. Not the music, not the scholarships, not the standing ovations.

Now it's bloodlines.

Followed by bullets.

Rocco's hand stays firm over my mouth, but his other hand strokes the side of my face like I'm a child on the edge of a nightmare. The tenderness rattles me. I don't understand it, but I cling to it like driftwood in a hurricane.

His voice comes low, steady, and deep, cutting through the chaos.

"Listen, Mia Lucia. You are not going to die. I won't allow it."

My breath hitches.

"That gunfire?" he continues, voice gravel and steel. "It's my men returning fire. Leo's soldiers are dead men walking. But we have to move. I'm going to get you out of here. We'll go somewhere safe. But you have to listen to me and do exactly what I say—like a good girl. Do you understand?"

No. I don't. Not at all.

But I nod anyway.

Because I have no one else. No other truth to hold onto.

I'm lying on the floor of my husband's bedroom—
surrounded by shattered glass, blood, and promises I never
asked for. Outside this room, men are hunting me. Inside it,
the devil himself is whispering comfort in my ear.

And God help me... I believe him.

I nod again, slower this time. Controlled.

Rocco watches me. Reading me and calculating the risk.
Then, slowly, he lifts his hand from my mouth. I don't
scream. I don't make a sound. I'm too focused on the one
thing that's keeping me tethered to reality: him.

He raises a single finger to his lips.

Silence.

I mimic the gesture and hold my breath. The gunfire has
stopped—but Rocco's body stays rigid, his movements
cautious. He doesn't know who won. Neither do I.

So, I lie there in the cradle of chaos, waiting for a verdict
neither of us can hear yet. And I tell myself:

Be a good girl.

Be quiet.

Survive.

"Alright, Lucia," Rocco says, voice low but commanding,
"we're going to crawl out of here and head for the stairs. Stay
flat, quiet, and on your belly if you need to, hold on to my
ankle while I move. I don't know what the smoke's like out
there, but I'm sure it's thick. And I'll be damned if you suffo-
cate on my watch. Nod if you understand."

I shake my head, more out of panic than defiance. The
tears won't stop, hot and unchecked.

He leans in and wipes one away with his thumb, then
presses a kiss just beneath my eye.

It's soft. Startling. Gentle, where everything else has been hard.

"Don't worry, fireball," he murmurs, the nickname curling around my fear like a flame. "This is just a moment. When I have you safe again, I swear, you will never feel fear like this. And whoever dared come for you tonight... will die by a thousand slow cuts. One for every tear they made you shed."

It's brutal. Terrifying.

And exactly what I need to hear.

Because right now, I need to believe this man would burn the world down to keep me breathing.

He slides off me and drops into a controlled crawl. Before he moves, he glances back and raises a finger to his lips again.

Silent. Stay low. Stay with me.

I grab his ankle like he said, and we begin our slow retreat into the unknown.

The hallway greets us with a choking mix of smoke and blood, hot metal and something coppery that sticks in the back of my throat. My lungs revolt. I cough, harsh and uncontrollable. I curse myself for the sound.

"It's okay," he calls out roughly. "Stay low. Keep going."

He rises to a crouch, draws a gun from the small of his back, and sweeps the hallway with trained efficiency. A white handkerchief appears in his hand, and he covers his mouth as he scans. Then he turns back.

"Clear. For now." His voice drops again, all steel and ice. "Looks like my cousin just wanted to rattle the cage. If he wanted us dead, he'd be here watching me carve his name into the floor with his spine."

He kneels beside me, presses the handkerchief to my mouth.

"Breathe through this. Shallow, slow. I'm going to carry you out to the car once we get downstairs. Keep your eyes on my back. Don't look around. I don't know how many bodies are outside this corridor—and I'd rather not have you vomiting all over my suit."

My stomach lurches anyway.

Bodies.

People are dead.

Because of me.

I nod, dazed—and then it hits me. I'm in nothing but a robe. No bra. No panties. My cheeks flame, panic blooming again.

Before I can speak, Rocco's eyes flick down, then back up—reading me like a book I didn't mean to open.

"Don't worry, wife," his voice is sharp. Final.

"No one will look. They know if they do, I'll rip their eyes out and shove them down their throats."

Well then.

So much for modesty.

"Stay to the walls," he barks over his shoulder as he slinks through the hallway like a panther, fast and silent. I follow his movements with wide, fearful eyes—until we hit the staircase.

And that's when I see it.

A body sprawled across the landing. Half a face.

Gone.

I gag. My knees buckle.

"Easy, piccola ragazza," he murmurs, suddenly beside me. "This is what I was trying to spare you. Come to me."

Before I can blink, I'm scooped into his arms. He pulls me in tight, pressing my face to his chest like I'm something precious, breakable.

Rocco takes the stairs fast and silently, and I let him. I want no part of the hell we're leaving behind. A few days ago, my life was music, laughter, and love. Now it's death in doorways and strangers dying because of the blood in my veins.

And I'm not angry at Rocco.

I'm not even angry at Leo.

I'm furious at my mother.

She should've told me who my father was. She should've prepared me for this life. Instead, she left like a thief in the night, and now I'm the one paying the price. I might never forgive her for that.

"Boss, they got all three of ours. But we dropped ten of theirs," Mario's voice cuts through the smoke like a blade. "No tats, no Ricci ink. No oaths. Just paid muscle. Mercs."

Ten bodies. God. They're out here somewhere—limbs twisted, eyes wide, blood soaking the concrete.

I feel Rocco tense beneath me. Then his palm presses harder to the back of my head, shielding me from it all.

His voice drops, low and lethal.

"Fuck."

"We shouldn't have lost anyone. Leo shouldn't have found this place so fast. What the fuck, Mario? I pay Enzo a goddamn fortune to make sure this doesn't happen."

His fury rolls off him in waves, vibrating through his chest, seething into my skin. It's not just anger—it's betrayal. And beneath it... blame. Rocco feels responsible. Like his life, the lives of his men were his to protect, and he failed.

We move again—fast. I hear Mario speak, muffled words I don't catch, followed by the sharp click of a car door.

Rocco doesn't stop.

He carries me straight to whatever getaway vehicle his crew prepped for nights like this. His arms never loosen. Not once.

And as the door opens for us, I know we've left something behind on that stairwell—

Our illusions.

Our safety.

My old life.

Forever.

"I know, boss. But it's not what you think," Mario says the second the car door shuts. "Enzo's convinced this wasn't Leo. I just spoke to him. He swears we've got eyes on him twenty-four-seven."

Rocco slides into the backseat with me still cradled in his lap like I'm something breakable. I try to sit up, but he doesn't let me—not yet. The back door shuts, and the driver's side opens with a creak as Mario slips behind the wheel.

He starts explaining himself.

And I already know it won't matter.

Rocco isn't the type to care about excuses. He's the kind to bleed you for wasting his time.

"Mario," Rocco growls, voice like ice cracking over fire, "you've got sixty seconds to tell me who just blew up my safe house... or I'll paint this overpriced Bentley in your fucking brain matter. You love this car so much? It would be a shame to die in it."

The engine roars to life as Mario speeds off into the night like nothing's wrong. Meanwhile, Rocco presses a kiss to the top of my head like the world isn't on fire. His hold on me loosens just enough for me to sit upright if I want to. I do, shifting slightly—just enough to breathe—but I stay on his lap.

He notices. Of course he does.

And that smug, shit-eating grin he gives me?

Infuriating.

He knows I'm choosing to stay close.

Not because I want him. Because I'm scared.

God, I hope he understands the difference.

Hell, I hope I do.

"There's no need to splatter my skull all over your fancy upholstery," Mario mutters, eyes on the road. "All I'm saying is Enzo's team has Leo locked. He's in New York sniffing around Ricci, not making moves here. Whoever hit us had inside intel—real-time. That safe house was as secure as Fort Knox. Cleaner than a Vatican ledger. The damn President doesn't sleep that securely."

Rocco lets out a low, humorless laugh and leans back, still holding me.

"Yet the White House still has a front door, Mario. My safe house doesn't."

"Not yet, anyway," Mario mutters.

I glance up, catching Mario's reflection in the rearview mirror. He's eerily calm. Like the threat of having his head blown off is just another item on tonight's agenda.

And Rocco? He's no longer tense either.

As if *this*—death threats, explosions, blood on the carpet —is just business as usual.

This is how they operate, how they breathe.

Violence is their air.

Loyalty, their religion.

And I'm strapped into the backseat of a bulletproof Bentley with the high priest and his sword arm.

No one tells you what it's like to be hunted.

No one tells you how fast survival warps everything you believe about right, wrong, and the space in between.

And no one warned me what it would feel like to stay in a killer's lap and be grateful for it.

When I shift in Rocco's lap to get comfortable his cock stiffens beneath me. He pulls me closer and nips at my neck before continuing his conversation with Mario. The gesture surprises me, but it's a nice one. I still hate him for making me marry him, but there's something to be said about the joy of knowing how much a man like him wants you.

Once he's satisfied with whatever mark he's left on my skin, he licks the spot to soothe the sting and continues speaking.

"So, what you're saying is that I must flush out a rat on top of everything else I need to do for this plan to work?"

Mario hits the gas, and we speed into the night. I look out

the window and see nothing but trees. It doesn't even seem that anyone else is out on the road. No one is chasing us, so what's the hurry?

"No, boss, you don't. The only men who knew about that safe house were the three guarding it; I made sure of that.

They didn't even know where they were going until an hour before they had to arrive. That's the same protocol I use with you, so there is no chance of a leak. All three guards are dead."

Rocco nods. "I see. But we still need to find out who the disloyal bastard was. Their friends and acquaintances may have information about who they were talking to. I want the name in 24 hours."

Mario clears his throat. "Yes, boss. It could be Ricci. Maybe he got wind that we have his daughter and didn't take too kindly to it."

My husband's hands tightly squeeze around my waist.

"I doubt that. Ricci has no idea I even know Lucia exists. He would suspect Leo or my uncle, not me. If you have eyes on Leo, so does he. He knows Leo doesn't have her. Maybe Leo used a decoy to throw us off. Like a taunt. That's his style."

Mario makes a sharp turn, and I almost fall off Rocco's lap. He catches me and yells at Mario. "Attento idiota!"

"Well, maybe you should put your precious cargo down in a seat of her own instead of holding her like a toddler."

Rocco jerks his body forward to retaliate, but I hold him steady. I do not want to come between these two men. First off, they're family. Second, I'd like to have Mario on my side, not against me. I don't want him to think of me as a nuisance.

I scoot off Rocco's lap and buckle myself into the seat next to him. I ignore his scowl and attempt to talk through the charged moment.

"It's all right Fieri. Mario is right. He's trying to get us to safety. The last thing he needs is me flying through his windshield."

Rocco slams his hand against the window so hard I'm surprised it doesn't break. "Don't call me Fieri again. I'm your husband, not some stranger. The next time, there will be consequences. The kind that requires you to bend over my knee in front of whoever witnesses the transgression!"

I stare at the monster I married and don't say a word. His mood swings are vicious. Shit! I can't believe I let him touch me, or that I wanted to touch him. This is a moment I must never forget. He is my enemy.

"I decide what Mario does and doesn't need, not you. What he needs to do is keep his thoughts about what I do with you to himself and get us to the airport in the next ten minutes. The pilot is waiting."

His tone snaps me back to reality. This man is a gangster, not a loving protector. But that's the least of my worries. Where is he taking me?

"Airport?" I ask. "Where are we going, and why? I know things are dangerous right now, but I was hoping. I could at least make some of my upcoming performances, with enhanced security, of course."

Rocco laughs and reaches out to stroke my cheek. "Oh,

my piccola ragazza. I forgot how naïve you are. You can never perform on a stage at that level again.

That's way too much exposure. That part of your life is over. What you must focus on now is your future."

I reach up and snatch his hand away. "And what kind of future can I possibly have with you? A man who dates death daily."

He shrugs. "A future full of danger, yes. But also passion, luxury, and the love of our children. You will live the life of a queen. Your training begins as soon as we board my private plane to my villa in Ravello, off Italy's Amalfi Coast."

I squirm to take my seat belt off as we approach the airstrip. Then I panic. As long as we were in the United States, I felt comfortable thinking that. I could ask for help, given the chance. Now, he wants to take me to a foreign country where I don't even speak the language? I will depend on him.

Hello no.

"Italy! I'm not going anywhere else with you! Let me out of this car right now!"

I try to open the door, but the locks are engaged. I scream and kick at him. But he catches my foot and squeezes, stilling me for a moment.

He shakes his head in disappointment. "No, I will not let you go. I did not want to do this, but if you can't cooperate, I must drug you again for your safety."

"I hate you!" I scream and whine, but he pulls me to him and pushes my head against his shoulder. When I feel the needle he must have had in his pocket, puncture the back of my neck, I release a silent cry.

The last thing I hear before I black out is his quiet words of advice against my ear.

"Prepare yourself la mia piccola palla di fuoco. Life with me will not be easy, but it will be worth it."

I doubt that very much.

11

ROCCO

Ravello is just as I remember.

Quiet, wealthy, and romantic.

The stone walls, white-washed Duomo, and cobbled streets make even the most hardened men feel sane.

Amalfi's hidden jewel is the only place I dare to call safe.

I hid here for an entire year after Matteo Ricci ruthlessly killed my parents in our home in Bari. Ravello was my uncle's idea. His enemies knew I escaped, and he was paranoid they would cut out what they left of his heart. My mother was his entire world. He never recovered from her death.

Some think that's why my uncle Thomasso is so unforgiving and hard. Those people don't know him. If they did, they'd recognize he was always a savage.

After my mother's death, he just stopped camouflaging his true ferocity. There was no point. He had zero fucks to give except for the fuck he gave when he took me under his wing.

He offered me refuge and saved my life. I owe him everything, including the Ricci throne on a silver platter.

I came to him as a shipwrecked sixteen-year-old. The
Ricci's hit us hard, and took away the two most important
people in my life. They tortured me and crushed my fingers
before I could escape, ensuring I'd never play piano again.

Then my uncle brought me here to a seaside village
known for its international music festivals. It felt like a cruel
joke. But after a month of living on the mountainside and
working in nearby Scala's lemon groves, I realized it kept my
mind sober.

When the time came to join Uncle Thomasso and the
family in Chicago, I could do so without bloodlust clouding
my judgment. Ravello was my salvation, and that's why I've
brought Lucia here.

Five years ago, I began renovations on an 800-year-old
villa that was once turned into a hotel during the 1930s. I
paid the owners a substantial amount of money to relinquish
their tourist business and turned Villa Dal Mare into my very
own 13,000-square-foot sanctuary. It's secluded and secure.

I did not create it with a woman in mind, but I expect the
home will be to Lucia's liking. I've only known her for a short
while, but I think the mix of vintage Italian and beach
modern decor will please her.

I just need her to wake up and see it.

She was still asleep when we landed in Naples this morning. My local driver, Canon, picked us up, and I held her
tightly in my arms for the entire commute.

When I first took her, I thought only of my uncle's needs.
My plan was to break her down into whatever my family and

I needed to ascend the throne that Leo aims to claim as his own—a throne with two seats: the Romanos and the Riccis. We've peacefully coexisted for the past twenty years, and none of that needs to change. The last war took too many precious lives; my mother's included. However, there can only be one leader, even in times of peace.

My uncle will become the don of all dons through this forced marriage

Kidnapping and matrimony are less bloody, but just as persuasive as a street offensive.

After making Lucia come last night, I witnessed a different side of her. She's responsive to my touch. She responds well to my... preferences. After I spanked her sweet ass, the first night we met, she was dripping wet, though she will never admit it.

She's mine.

Thinking about how I will punish her for acting out and throwing a tantrum in the car while we escaped makes my dick hard. I hated to drug her, but she was raving, and the adrenaline was wearing off. I didn't want her to deal with the crash on a plane 30,000 feet in the air. I'd do that and more to keep her safe. There was nothing I could do to save my mother, but I will not fail Lucia.

I never wanted a wife, but now that I have one, you can be damn sure I'll die before I let anyone harm her.

She's mine.

It's been twelve hours since I put her to sleep, and now I'm eager for her to wake. When we arrived at Dal Mare, I stripped her of her robe and laid her beautiful body bare on my 1000 thread count Egyptian sheets. I pray it's just the soft fabric keeping my little fireball asleep.

I've taken a shower and planned our dinner menu and wine for the evening. The house staff is prepared to see to Lucia's every whim once she's ready.

Mario and Enxo are looking into who attacked us. I still suspect Leo, but Mario's convinced it's not him. He asked for another twenty-four hours to shake some trees in person and on the dark web. Someone will know something, or die trying to keep the secret.

Mario can be very convincing.

There's nothing left for me to do but sit on the bed beside Lucia and wait.

I pick up the book I left on my bedside stand when I was here six months ago, *Jane Eyre*. The previous owners left the book in the villa, and it intrigued me. The scene where Mr. Rochester meets Jane for the first time captivates me. Jane bewitches his horse, much like Lucia has bewitched my icy heart. But she will never fully own it.

I'm not built for love. But I can protect her and make sure that the rest of her days are comfortable. She will want for nothing as long as she doesn't want for love.

I turn the page, and she mumbles and stirs somewhere between sleep and consciousness.

"Rocco... please.... please...," her sweet voice pleads.

The whimpers make my cock stir. It's likely that she's dreaming about the orgasm I gave her in the shower last night after making her my wife. I'm upset that our wedding night was interrupted by violence. However, tonight that won't happen. I'm making Lucia completely mine, with no exceptions.

When her arms thrash and her body jerks, I worry. She's having a terror.

"No, mommy. Please don't leave me. Don't go...!" she screams.

I put my book down, gently shake her awake, and pull her into my arms. "It's alright, Lucia, I'm here. Wake up, little one."

For a moment, she nuzzles against my chest to accept the comfort my body offers. It's the first touch she's given me without coercion. She may be semi-conscious, but often that is where our genuine desires hide. But as quickly as the moment starts, it ends.

Lucia jumps up with a gasp, opening and closing her eyes repeatedly to adjust to the light. When she can see, she rubs her head and looks up at me. A flicker of relief floats over her face for the briefest moment. She's glad it's me and not the men who were shooting at us yesterday. I'm all she needs in the world to survive for thirty precious seconds. But once she realizes she's safe and remembers the last twenty-four hours, she shuts her features and gives me a look that could kill.

"Tell me, Fieri." Her hoarse voice is as harsh as a full-throated scream. "Will you ever tire of drugging and kidnapping me?"

I smirk. "Yes. When you learn to trust and obey me like a good girl."

She rolls her eyes and rubs her throat. The drugs made her throat dry like before, but I'm prepared. I reach over and grab the pitcher of lavender-infused water my staff readied at my request. I pour the cool water into a crystal glass and hand it to her. When our hands touch, a noticeable spark flies between us.

She snatches the glass and murmurs a thank you. After drinking the contents in its entirety, she hands the glass to me with a chilled glare.

"If you want me to trust you, stop drugging and dragging me at your whim. The only thing I can trust is that you will do exactly what you want to Rocco, without taking a moment's thought of what anyone else may want or need."

My muscles tense. She wants a fight, and I should avoid her trap. It won't help our situation in the long run. But my body vibrates with a mixture of lust and pure anger. How can she say these words with a straight face? Less than twenty-four hours ago, I covered her body, prepared to take a bullet for her ungrateful ass.

She turns to move, but before she can run away, I pin her back to the bed and grab her jaw. When I straddle her thighs, she inhales a sharp breath.

Good, be afraid.

For my dramatic pleasure, I lean down and growl against her skin. She smells incredible. Her vanilla scent is an aphrodisiac.

"Ohhhh Lucia, you don't believe that. Your safety is always my top priority, as I've proven over the past few days. Will I ask your fucking opinion when it comes to keeping you alive? No, I will not. You will be a good girl and do what I say, or face my belt against your ass. Your obedience is non-negotiable."

I kiss the side of her right cheek before dragging my lips down to her collarbone and biting down on the soft flesh. When she winces, I replace the sharp pinch with the softness of my tongue and circle where I nipped. The delicious moan released from her lips is a minor victory.

As I repeat my kiss, bite, and lick on her left side, I whisper. "I owe you a punishment for your behavior in the car. I told you to do exactly what I said before we left the safe house. Yet the moment the gunfire stopped and you thought the immediate danger had passed, you threw a tantrum. A tantrum so large that I had to drug you for your safety. Now, a lesson must be taught."

She scrambles to push me off, but she doesn't make any gains. I'm easily 100 pounds heavier than her, and it's all muscle. She's not going anywhere until I want her to. The quicker she submits to me, the faster we can enter into a marriage of not just convenience, but also consistency. I can't keep going like this. Her mood swings affect my concentration. She needs to understand her place soon.

"Fuck you." See hisses between clenched teeth. It's muffled, but I understand the disrespectful sentiment perfectly. She will pay dearly for the words.

I lift my body off hers, and she rolls away like she's escaped my grasp. I've gone about her training all wrong. We're married, but it won't mean a thing if she doesn't implicitly obey me. Trust will come later when she realizes I mean what I say, and that I will never lie to her.

If I say she will be punished, she will be punished.

If I say that she deserves an orgasm, she will come until she blacks out.

If I fucking tell her that the moon will hide tomorrow night, then you better believe it's going to be pitch black outside.

She will trust no one's words, actions, or touch but mine. In a world as violent as ours, that is imperative.

Her training starts now.

Casually, I stand and block her sight of the only exit. She won't be leaving until I say so.

"Are you hungry?" I know she's starving, but I also expect the answer she gives me.

"No, I'm fine; however, I would like my cellphone. May I have it now?"

I take a deep breath. "You will get your phone back when I can trust you with it. Now, you need to eat, especially after the drug you've ingested. I don't want you to get sick."

She laughs. "Oh, so now you're worried about my health? You're the one who stuck the needle in my neck."

She jumps off the bed and paces, working herself into a frenzy. I know if I don't do something soon, she really will make herself sick.

"Take me back to America this instant. I want to return to my apartment and my life. If we were under attack at your safe house, that means I'm not safe anywhere. If my death is inevitable, I'd rather die in the comfort of my home than be trapped here with you."

"Inevitable?!" I bark. When I move closer to her and she steps back.

"Are you suggesting that I can't keep you safe? I will slit the throat of any man that even tries to touch you. You don't know who the fuck I am."

She swallows hard and continues to walk backwards as I stalk her up against a wall." Rocco," she quietly pleads.

I chuckle at her trapped state. "I am the biggest demon in hell, sweetheart. The fuckers that attacked us are dead. And the man that sent them will soon meet the same fate."

As soon as I figure out who the fuck it is...

I reach out and twirl a curl of her hair around my finger before smiling up at her. "The only inevitable thing in this equation is your full obedience and my dominance of your body. You are mine, Lucia, but you seem to be the last one to understand your position. Allow me to help you comprehend."

The smell of her fear turns me on. I know I'm a sick bastard, but no one will harm a hair on her head. If it takes a heavy hand to keep her safe, so be it. She's trembling before me, but I'm ravenous.

"Why-what... how?" Lucia mumbles. The swift movement of my hand flips her around until her face is against the wall. She's still naked, a fact I think she must have forgotten. Maybe I'll keep her like this. Her soft and inviting body is mine for the taking whenever I want. Her hunger for me is apparent by the smell of her arousal. She likes control. She craves domination.

I land four quick and heavy swats on her bare ass and almost come in my pants when I hear her choke back a moan. "Stop... please..." she pleads.

"Stop, my fireball? Stop spanking your ass and making you wet for me? Or do you want me to stop giving you what you need to survive this ordeal?"

I smack her twice more and smile at the blushing shade of red that appears on her ample ass.

"This power struggle sets us back, Lucia. There's no need for it. You will obey, and you have nothing to worry about except how I will please you."

"Oh My God," she wails when I land two more swats on her ass before swiping my finger through her drenched pussy. Repeatedly, I rub until her knees buckle. She rides my fingers until I take them away.

"Unh Unh Unh," I whisper against her ear. "Naughty girls don't get to come. Did my hand on your ass make your pussy greedy, Lucia? You want more, don't you?"

She shakes her head. "You're wrong. I don't want this."

I grab a handful of her hair, lean her head back on my shoulder, and bring my wet fingers up to her eyes to see.

"Oh, but you do, my Lucia. Taste how much you want this." I push my fingers into her mouth, and the little vixen licks them clean like a kitten lapping its milk. The swirl and suck of her tongue makes me think of how it will feel wrapped around my cock, but now is not the time to find out. She needs to eat.

I release my fingers from her mouth with a pop, and give both of her ass cheeks a gentle tap.

"I think you might need a reminder of who you belong to for the rest of the evening. Come with me."

I keep one hand behind her back and place my other hand around her neck to walk her to the bed. When we reach it, I toss her on the duvet and command her to stay.

"Don't move. If you do, I'll know, and you'll be punished; this time with my belt. You can't run, because there's nowhere for you to go. This estate is huge but wired. I will find you and take my disappointment out on that pretty little ass of yours. Understand?"

She glares at me but nods. I chuckle and walk over to my armoire and pull out a new pair of metal Ben Wa balls. Thai is just the thing to keep my wife tame during dinner. When I walk towards her, swinging the balls from my forefinger, her eyes widen and her breathing quickens.

"Wh-what are you going to do with those?"

I don't answer her. Instead, I slowly stalk towards her. "Open your mouth for me, piccola ragazza. You'll want to get these nice and wet before I stuff your pussy with them. Though I suspect you're already sufficiently wet."

Lucia clamps her legs shut and sits up. " I'm not wearing those. You're crazy."

I shake my head. "Lucia, we can either do this the easy way and insert these beautiful balls into your saturated pussy. Or, I can go and get a but plug for your untried ass, because we both know that no one has claimed that little hole yet. Either way, something of mine is going inside that gorgeous body of yours, to remind you who you belong to. Now, which will it be? I'd much rather you enjoy this, but that's up to you."

Her eyes would incinerate my soul if I had one. But since I don't, I find her anger cute. We both know that she belongs to me. She gave me the ownership rights that day in my safe-house's basement when I spanked her pretty ass over my knee.

She chose me then, and she will pick me now; my wait time is unparalleled.

Slowly, she opens those pretty thighs for me and lays her head down on the bed. She thinks she can hide from me, but I won't allow it. I slap her inner thighs, and she gasps. "Eyes on me, Lucia. I want you to see your greedy little pussy swallow up my favorite pair of balls."

"Bastard," she hisses, but obeys. I chuckle and wipe the fresh line of juices flowing down her quivering legs. She's so wet for me. My cock is painfully hard, but I control myself.

Never leaving her gaze, I insert one ball and then two. I push them deep, ensuring the top ball will hit her G-spot when she walks. She'll be a shaking, pleasurable mess by dinner, and that's my plan. When I'm done, I kiss her knees and bite one thigh. Her moan is a fucking praise.

"Now, be a good girl and put some clothes on. You have thirty minutes to take a shower and meet me downstairs in the kitchen. Don't remove the balls or touch your pussy and steal my orgasm. I'll know if you do and then my butt plug will be next. I have clothes for you in the closet. Don't be late, or I'll give you a real punishment. You won't come at all tonight and your pussy will be hungrier than it is now."

I push away from her and exit the room. When I leave, I hear her curse my name, but I'll let her have that. We have the rest of our lives for her to learn some respect.

12

ROCCO

The moment I shut the bedroom door, I seal a piece of my control behind it.

Lucia's in there—bound by my punishment, pulsing with frustration, and likely plotting her next rebellion.

And yet, all I can think about... is feeding her.

Pathetic.

I should be preparing for war, not heading into the kitchen like some smitten fool. But here I am, waving off Maria with a clipped, "Take the night off."

She pauses, surprised. I never cook for anyone.

But Lucia isn't anyone.

She's mine.

And tonight, she eats from my hands.

Every bite. Every sip. Every quiet moan of pleasure. All mine.

I move like a man possessed—knife flashing, flame roaring, basil and garlic perfuming the air. The same rhythm I learned at my mother's elbow when I was still just a boy with raw fingers from piano keys and a father whose bark outweighed his worth.

Back when music was my only rebellion.

Back when I still believed love didn't leave scars.

Cooking calmed me then. My mother would press dough into my hands and say, *"If you can feed someone, you'll never lose your humanity."*

Now these hands punish.

They dominate.

They carve obedience into the bodies of men—and bury pleasure into the softest parts of her.

Even after everything—her disobedience, her fire, the chaos she stirs in me—I want to nourish her.

I want to watch her lips wrap around the food I made, feel her sigh when the flavor hits her tongue, and know I put that sound in her throat.

God help me, I want her to crave me in every way.

That's the problem.

Lucia Ricci is a distraction—a storm wrapped in silk and attitude. Every minute I spend thinking about her is one I could be using to destroy Leo or secure our next move with Ricci.

But she's *in* me now.

And if I'm not careful, she'll become more than my weakness—she'll become my downfall.

No. I can't allow that. I've worked too long and killed too many. I'm not throwing it away for a beautiful, disobedient concert pianist with daddy issues and a mouth that makes me want to sin.

But... I'll feed her tonight.

And maybe—just maybe—if she looks at me with those eyes full of fire and surrender... I won't burn with her.

I place some garlic bread into the oven and rise to Enzo standing across the island from me with a raised eyebrow and a ridiculous smirk on his face. He was silent on the plane ride here, because he knew I was pissed. He wasn't scared of me; he was disappointed in himself. The man is a serial perfectionist.

Enzo is sharp and a certified genius. His father is still a soldier on Capo Richie Caruso's construction crew and has spent thirty years in the same position, as he gambles as much as he works. Regardless, Mickey Bianchi is a good man and highly respected within the family. He can kill a man with one punch. He was a professional boxer before becoming a made man, and he is vicious in the ring. He's Caruso's muscle, and he tried to teach both Mario and Enzo to have the same bloodthirst as him.

The problem was that Enzo never loved boxing the way his father did. Enzo would rather make his enemies suffer by draining their bank accounts or hacking into their lives to blackmail them. His torture is life-altering, and you don't want to be on his bad side. He's a vindictive son of a bitch, but he's loyal to his circle. He's also our comedian when he wants to be, but that shit gets old quick.

"When did you become Chef Boyardee? Should I get you an apron and hat to complete your look?"

I slam the oven shut with my foot and look up.

"Fuck off Enzo! I hope you have some information about who tried to kill my wife and me, along with your witty comments."

He nods, and his face turns solemn. "Indeed, I do. It was just as Mario and I thought, Leo had only just found out that Lucia was missing. He didn't have time to coordinate such an attack. It wasn't him, but he is still the reason for the attack."

When he pauses and crosses his arms, I'm ready to jump across the table and punch him in his smug face. "Well? How is Leo responsible, and who is behind the attack?"

He takes his time pulling out a stool to sit down. Enzo's theatrics piss me off and he knows it. He also knows that I'll wait. I can already tell that I will not like what he has to say, and that makes him cautious. Whenever he delivers bad news, he jokes and stalls to calm his nerves. It only makes me angrier.

"It appears we've been heavily surveilled for the past few years by the Riccis. They knew where the safe house was and when you entered it. They were the ones who attacked."

I pause.

This makes no sense.

I lean forward against the island with my elbows on the counter and get eye to eye with Enzo. "Tell me everything from the beginning and leave nothing out this time, Enzo. What the hell is going on?"

He straightens his impossibly long body on the stool and gets to the point. "Leo reached out to the Riccis and forecast his plans. He sent a ransom note before he secured Lucia, thinking it was a done deal. He dared Matteo Ricci to stop him."

"Fuck!" I curse under my breath.

Idiota! Leo was more interested in the show and threat than in being strategic about his plan. If it went south, he probably assumed his daddy would bail him out. He doesn't know my uncle is through with him.

Mario nods and walks to the island where Enzo and I are huddled. "Exactly, boss. Of course, he didn't share that he was going rogue on his little mission to extort Don Daddy Ricci. Therefore, Matteo assumed the Romanos were behind the threat. Since he already had men on us for normal surveillance, he asked about our movements. They told him we kidnapped a woman from Lucia's building. The three rats we killed weren't Leo's men. They were Matteo Ricci's."

Damn, this keeps getting worse. I nod, now understanding.

"So, the men claimed to be Leo's because that's what we wanted to hear, and because they would never give their boss up."

Enzo nods. "Once they reported to Matteo that we had Lucia, he sanctioned the attack. What happened at the Safehouse was a rescue attempt to save her life, not to kill her. Lucia's father wants her back."

I slam my hand on the marble counter. "That fucking parasite Leo always messes everything up! This was not the plan!"

At that moment, Mario walks in and looks over his shoulder towards the hallway. He knows I don't want Lucia to hear any of this. I motion towards the hallway. "In my office." Enzo nods and follows me. Mario joins us.

As we walk through the hallway, I walk past the stairs, and I look at my watch. She still has seven minutes. Part of me hopes she's late so I can punish her. Seeing her sweet ass jiggle with every swat of my hand makes me want to pull my flogger out to mark every inch of her lovely body. Her reactions to my hand make me think it's something she would also enjoy.

Once we're in my office, Enzo begins again. "When we contact Ricci, the conversation must be different. He needs to know why you have his daughter, and I guess now he also needs to know why you married her without his permission. I doubt we're going to convince him that this was for her safety when you could have just told him what was going on from the beginning."

I punch my fist down on my desk behind me. This is a clusterfuck, but it's fixable.

I lean against my desk as my mind races. I turn to Mario and smile,

"You know, this may be better."

Mario goes to the bar and pours himself a drink. The look on his face tells me he sincerely doubts that, but I continue anyway.

"Ricci knows I couldn't tell him the plan. I can't tell him about the Romano business. How could I trust he would be on our side? He would have moved the same way. The plan can still move forward. I already have his daughter, and she's already my wife. She's safe from Leo and in my care. If Matteo ever wants to see her again, he'll do what we say and help us take Leo down. If he kills Leo, Thomasso won't have to, and the family can save face. By this time tomorrow, Leo will know all that has transpired, and we will all be at war."

Enzo sighs, seeming to understand. He's probably upset he didn't think of it himself.

Mario knocks back his drink before speaking. "OK, that could work, but what about Lucia?"

"What about her?"

He holds his hands up in surrender. "I'm sure that part of the reason she's even tolerating you is that she thinks you saved her life and that you're her only option for safety. If her father is an actual option, how will you keep that information from her? Now you truly are keeping her as a pawn, and she may never forgive you."

I wave my hand in his direction and tut. "This isn't about forgiveness. We have a marriage of convenience, Mario. I don't care if she's pissed, her feelings are of little consequence to me. I have a job to complete. I'd also appreciate it if you leave my woman's feelings to me. It's none of your concern."

Mario glares but stays quiet. I know he's only trying to help, but I don't like anyone insinuating that I don't know how to take care of my wife or that I could lose her.

Enzo laughs to break the tension. "No disrespect, Roc, but I call bullshit. I'm your closest friend, and I know you. You're making your mother's homemade red sauce and pasta. You weren't just thinking about your wife as a business transaction, standing at the oven like your nonna. You've caught feelings for the girl. Just admit it. Only then can you shove them deep down in your belly and shit them out. Because you can't let that impede the end goal."

I stare at them both for a few seconds before I continue. When I speak, my voice is deadly quiet.

"We are all friends, but remember your place. When have I ever put my feelings over family? My uncle saved my life, and I will never let him down. I know what I must do for this family; do you? You keep your nose in Leo's business, and I'll handle mine. What Lucia doesn't know won't hurt her. There's no way for her father to get in touch with her without me, and she does not know he's looking for her. I'll reach out to Ricci and make it very clear what he can and cannot say to his daughter if he wants to keep her and his family intact. Then we can move to the next step and take Leo's sorry ass down."

"Enzo, in the meantime, keep Aria out of preschool and add extra soldiers to her security detail. Recheck her nanny's background, I don't want any surprises there." I look up at Mario and see the appreciation in his eyes. That little girl means the world to all of us. What he doesn't understand is that I'd give my life for her. She's our treasure.

I look down at my watch and see I only have two minutes to spare.

"I need to go." I stalk out of my office and slam the door behind me.

I want to be in the kitchen when she arrives. The thought reminds me that Enzo was not too far off in his warnings. I care, and I need to kill that quickly.

Lucia is my wife, but she's just a means to an end. I can't afford to fall in love or have any distractions from my family's ascension. She's only a pawn—hopefully, an obedient one.

It's time for another lesson in submission.

Her total surrender is the only way we both survive.

13

LUCIA

Am I Rocco's wife... or hostage?

It's becoming increasingly difficult to distinguish between the two.

I should be plotting my escape and making plans. Resisting the pull of the man who drugged me, spanked me, and ripped me away from everything I've ever known.

But here I am—wrapped in luxury, breathing in his cologne, and wondering how it's possible to hate someone so much and still want them every time they walk into the room.

Rocco Fieri is not a hero.

He's a captor with a code.

A savage wrapped in silk, and I hate how safe I feel near him.

Yes, he's kept me alive. Yes, he's given me a taste of what it's like to be truly claimed—body and soul—and I can't forget that one devastating orgasm that nearly rewired my entire nervous system. But that's not reason enough to surrender. Right?

And yet... if I run, where the hell would I go?

Leo's still out there, hunting me like I'm his favorite toy that got stolen. And now, thanks to some twisted Mafia inheritance I never asked for, I'm the viral sensation of the criminal underworld. According to what I overheard from Rocco's phone calls—yes, I was awake—my name is bouncing across the dark web like a damn bidding war. I'm not just Ricci's daughter anymore. I'm currency. Leverage. A trophy with a price tag in blood.

So, no. I'm not safe.

Not in this house.

Not in my skin.

Not even in my head.

Sometimes I close my eyes and pretend my father will show up, guns blazing, to rescue me. It's a nice fantasy. Matteo Ricci is powerful enough. Respected enough. But the truth? He's known about me for twenty-four years and did precisely nothing.

No birthday calls.

No secret meetings.

Not even a single, fucking postcard.

When I was eight, there was a father-daughter dance at school. I asked my mom why I didn't have a dad. She smiled, as if her heart was breaking, and told me he was lost to the wind. I thought that meant he was dead.

He isn't. He's just... absent. By choice.

My mom, on the other hand? She *showed up*. She found a kind doctor, Dr. Norris, who escorted me to that dance. And everyone after. He held my hand like it mattered. Like I mattered.

He died of a heart attack eight years ago, and I haven't thought about a father figure since.

So no, I don't believe Matteo Ricci is coming for me.

Not now. Not ever.

And that leaves me with exactly one option:

Rocco Fieri.

A man who burns when he looks at me.

Who touches me like he owns every inch of skin.

Who terrifies me—and makes my body betray me every time he's near.

He's dangerous. He's brutal. He's controlling.

But he's also the only person in this entire blood-soaked nightmare who has made me feel... protected.

I don't know what that makes me.

A wife?

A fool?

Or just a survivor clinging to the most dangerous lifeline in the room.

I walk over to a wall of windows and take a deep breath. The balls he inserted inside me are working my body over. Every step is like a caress to my inner walls, and it takes me a few minutes of practice not to falter with every step. I won't give him the satisfaction of seeing me succumb to his sexual torture.

The view outside the bedroom window is breathtaking. If I weren't here against my will, I would call it romantic. Maybe that's why he brought me here? A romantic gesture of some sort.

Rocco is like Jekyll and Hyde. One minute he's attentive and caring for my needs, then the next he's threatening me with soft-core violence. Just the thought of his rumbling voice earlier in my ear makes me shiver.

You will be a good girl and do what I say or face my belt against your ass. Your obedience is non-negotiable.

The nerve of the man is astonishing. However, I don't doubt his words. If there's one thing I've learned about my new husband, it's that he means what he says. His follow-through is unmatched. I need to cooperate until I can figure out a way to get free. It won't do me any good to push his buttons.

I'll start by arriving at dinner on time.

The shower is spacious and features a white and gold marble design. The hot water and steam are just what my aching bones and muscles need. I didn't realize how much of an effect the last 72 hours had on me. Escaping the safe house traumatized my mind, body, and spirit, and I never want to be that close to death again.

I take a deep breath as jets of water hit me from behind. A rainfall showerhead douses my body in water from above, making me feel brand new. A girl could get used to a shower like this. The water pressure in my Bronx apartment is never strong enough, and there's barely enough space to turn around.

I want to come so bad that it hurts. He left me worked up and ready to explode. His strong hand slapping my ass does something to me.

It's a kink; I never knew I had.

Then he had to go and insert these damn balls, I'm

hanging on by a thread. But, I'll obey because there's no way in hell I'm letting him stuff anything in my ass.

After about 10 minutes of luxuriating, it's time to get out. There is a heated closet to the left of the shower, where I find warm towels. I grab one, dry off, and wrap the large towel around me. I tuck it close as I step into the walk-in closet.

Rocco didn't bother to get any of my clothes before he whisked me away. There's no telling what he's packed for me to wear. When I walk in, I'm pleasantly surprised to see row after row of soft cashmere sweaters, silk tank tops, white crisp button-up shirts, and comfortable jersey tops and dresses. Everything is in soft muted colors and neutrals. Exactly the things I would buy if I had disposable income to spend on clothes. How did he know?

Since it's a little warm, I chose a long black silk maxi dress that falls below my ankles. My eyes widen as I notice *Prada* written on the label. The price tag is still attached, and I gasp.

*$2150.*00

The foolishness that rich people spend their money on is beyond me.

That's an entire month of rent for my New York apartment. My Morris Heights neighborhood is known as Little Ghana, and even though our rent is controlled, it's still astronomical compared to what you get. But it's where my people are.

I lay the silk dress on the bed and head over to the dresser to find some underwear. Everything is neatly arranged, and the silk and lace are so soft I purr. I put on a black thong and don't worry about a bra. My breasts aren't itty bitty, but they're not large either. My B cup gets me by. The neckline of this dress looks fantastic. The V-neck accentuates my cleavage in the best possible way.

Back in the bathroom, I look into the vanity mirror and realize my hair is just fine as it is. The shower steam made it damp enough to curl up on its own. Now it's a big, soft, curly plume of hair. A few passes with the diffuser define my curls, and I'm happy.

I almost jumped with glee when I saw Fenty makeup products lined up in one of the vanity drawers. One swipe of Fenty lip bomb gloss and mascara is just enough. A spritz of some lemon perfume that apparently is native to this area is the final touch, and I'm ready to meet my master.

I halfway expect to find the bedroom locked before I remember he instructed me to meet him downstairs. Outside the bedroom, my senses perk up. There's a sea breeze fragrance flowing throughout the beautiful villa. A landing is located right outside the main bedroom, providing a 360-degree view of the entire second floor. I can also look down from the balcony and see straight through to the first.

He decorated the home in wonderful pale shades of white, sand, and gold with blue accents. There are numerous plants, rock accents, and seascapes on the walls. This isn't a place I'd expect a harbinger of death to live. This home is full of life and every good thing that God provides us on earth. The contradiction is unsettling.

I head down the stairs, following the unmistakable smell of garlic and tomatoes. My mouth waters, and my stomach growls. His cook must be making some sort of pasta. Maybe he's in his office or something, and I can chat with his cook before dinner. I could use a few more moments before facing him. She may give me more information about my enigmatic spouse.

I put on a bright smile and walk into the kitchen, expecting to find an elderly Italian woman cooking up a storm. Instead, I find my husband wearing a tight white T-shirt and gray sweatpants hanging low on his hips. He's stirring the pot of sauce in time with the Hazel Scott piano rift, blasting from his speakers. His muscles flex as he stirs, and his hips sway slightly to the beat. I stay quiet and enjoy a rare look at my husband unbound.

I clear my throat. Then he turns around and flashes me a smile.

A fucking smile.

It's genuine. The kind that reaches his eyes. It's the first one he's given me since we met. He's relaxed and in his element. This place must be his real home.

I run my hands along the spaghetti straps on my dress, suddenly self-conscious as he peruses me from head to toe. I need to speak, or I'll spontaneously combust from his heated stare alone. He must have taken a shower because his hair is still damp, and the thick black strands are curling. The man is sex on a stick, and I need to distract myself before I jump on said stick.

"I love Hazel Scott." I blurt out.

He smirks, turns back around, and places a top on his sauce. He wipes his hand on a dish towel hanging on the stove before turning back around to lean against it and face me.

"I know you do. That's why I'm playing her music for you."

Is there anything this man doesn't know about me? With his resources, he probably has an entire dossier on me. What else does he know? My phone password? My guilty pleasure of ordering pralines from that Savannah Candy shop - I love it. The type of porn I watch when I'm lonely at night? The last thought causes my cheeks to heat. That would be a disaster.

He chuckles. "Relax, Lucia. It was a lucky guess. You're a concert pianist. It only makes sense that you would love one of the most prolific female pianists of all time. I didn't break into your Apple Music playlist."

A small sigh of relief escapes my lips. I take a seat on one stool at the bar across from him. The kitchen is as stunning as he is. It's an ode to white and gold marble. Even the appliances are a soft champagne gold color. He must have had them custom-made. I look down at the white and gold granite of the bar and smile at the amount of sparkle. I look up at Rocco as he studies me with curiosity, and I clear my throat once again.

"I didn't think you paid attention to what I do or love."

He shrugs. "I'm not a monster."

I throw him an incredulous look, and he raises his hands in surrender.

"Ok, I'm not a *total* monster. Just a bit monstrous." He shrugs and turns to pop a cherry tomato from the counter in his mouth. I don't know how he made a gesture so simple, sexy as hell, but he did.

"But Lucia, I have no desire to be that way with you.

You're my wife, and if you're a good girl for me, I think you will find me a very generous lover in every sense of the word. So yes, I pay attention to you, and I admire your skill on the piano."

I shift my stance and cross my arms to eye him warily. "You've heard me play?"

He runs his hand over the five o'clock shadow covering his face.

God, even his scruff is sexy.

"I may have looked up a few of your performances on YouTube. You're good."

I blush. "I'm alright. There are so many more pianists who are better than I am. Before I was... taken. They ranked me in the top fifty worldwide."

"There are not forty-nine musicians better than you, wife. And I'm not just saying that either. I know more about the piano than you think. At one point in my life, I held recitals all over this country. I even played in the orchestra pit of Teatro Massimo for a performance of Aida when I was fifteen years old. My mother was also a concert pianist before she died."

My jaw drops. This can't be real. There's no way this man plays the piano at that level. If he did, why the hell is he in the mafia now?

What happened to him?

He laughs. "Close your mouth la mia piccola palla di fuoco. Am I such a Neanderthal? You can't believe that I was an accomplished musician? Do you think I was born a criminal?"

I shake my head. "No, that's not it. If you say you were a

concert pianist, then you were. You're not a liar. You've been very honest with me about my circumstances, and I appreciate that."

He gives me a funny look before turning away and stirring his sauce.

"Let's eat. I've made my Nonna's famous red sauce and orecchiette. Meet me in the dining room. I'll come soon."

His voice is gruff, and I'm not sure what changed his mood. Maybe I offended him? That's not how I wanted to turn over a new leaf with him.

I rise from the bar and head towards what I assume is the dining room. Before I get to the arched doorway, I stop. "Rocco, I apologize if I offended you. I'm just shocked that you appreciate music, since you forbade me from playing ever again."

Rocco puts the wooden spoon down with a loud smack on the stove. Within seconds, he's in front of me with his hands on my shoulders.

"Lucia, I did not forbid you to play because I hate or don't appreciate music. I forbade you to play because it's not safe for you to be in public. I thought I made that clear."

He runs his hands up and down my arms. "I love your talent, and I have a grand piano here. I have two, so please play whenever you like. Hopefully, when this is all over, we can find a way for you to perform, but I make no promises. You will always be a high security risk. I want you to know that I respect your art and intimately understand the sacrifice you're making."

I suck in a deep breath. Hearing him say these words takes my anxiety down a few notches.

"OK, I'd like to play for you." I place a hand on his chest. "Will you return the gesture and play for me one day?"

He takes my hand off his chest and kisses the inside of my palm. "No Lucia, I no longer play for others."

I look him in his eyes. "Never? Why? If it's something you loved and were good at before the mafia claimed, you. Why quit it?"

A shadow falls over his face. "That's none of your business. My past is not something I talk about. The why doesn't matter. Just know that I don't play and will not play again. Now, be a good girl and have a seat for me at the table."

I want to push back and get to the root of the issue, but I decide not to. Instead, I follow directions like a good little slave. His mood swings are too much to keep up with, and I'm hungry.

The rest of the dinner is uneventful. Rocco is an excellent cook, and he looks pleased when I polish off two bowls of the tasty dish. We keep our conversation light. I am dying to have an update on this entire Leo situation and who bombed the safe house. But I know that will be a dead end.

Instead, we stick to facts about Amalfi and all the things he will show me over the next few days. He even shares the history of the Barese women like his Nonna, who are known for their orecchiette. They make it from scratch and sell it illegally in the streets of Bari. The history is fascinating.

When he takes our bowls away, I stretch. "So what's for dessert?"

He walks over and offers his hand. As I take it, he leans over and whispers, "You are."

"Wh-wh-at," I stammer.

He smirks. "You heard me. Strip naked and lie back on the dining table. Present your pussy to me. I want to see how juicy my balls have left your sweet cunt."

His dirty words warm me from the inside out. I hesitate, and he frowns. I know he wants quick and unequivocal obedience.

If I obey him, he will make me feel good.

If I don't, I will be punished.

It's that simple.

Or is it? I've never stripped for a man before, and certainly not in a dining room. However, this feels like a defining moment. Either I'm going to trust Rocco, or I'm not. Stripping when he tells me to is a small test that I really want to pass. So, I do it.

I pull down one strap of the silk dress and then the other before shimmying out of the rest of my dress. When I'm standing in nothing but my lace thong, my instinct is to cover my naked breasts, but I remember his words from our wedding night.

You are never to hide from me, Lucia. Your body is my reward. Do you understand?

I stand tall and push my shoulders back. My boldness grows, and my nipples harden as he looks at me with a hungry glare. He gestures to my pussy with his fingers, and I snatch my thong down.

"Come." The single command causes my body to shiver.

Rocco holds his hand out for me and lifts me onto the dining room table. I look around, nervous that anyone could come in here, but he tsks.

"Don't worry, beautiful. No one else is home. I've given

them all the night off so I can feast on you in peace. Sit up for me."

Rocco grabs a clean table napkin and ties it around my eyes before laying me back down.

"First, I'm going to feast, and then I'm going to fuck you long and hard. When I'm done, you can play me something on my piano."

He doesn't give me a chance to respond. Instead, he places both his hands on my body, one on each of my thighs, and he spreads me wide. My knees hit the table, and my body becomes an open book. He leans down, takes a deep breath while sniffing my sex. It's the filthiest and most erotic thing I've ever heard in my life. Not being able to see only heightens my arousal, and I realize that was his plan the entire time.

When he presses down on the top of my sex, it makes the balls scrape against my walls, and I moan in pleasure. He chuckles before reaching in and pulling the balls out. He holds them in front of my face, and they're glistening with my arousal.

"Lick them clean." He orders. I'm so turned on that I do it without question. My sweet, musky scent makes me vibrate with even greater need. When I've licked them clean, he groans his approval and throws the balls over his shoulder before getting to work.

There are no gentle licks or swipes on my clit. Rocco dives in and tastes me from ass to clit and backs down again with strong, firm licks before placing his thumb and index finger on my nub to pinch. The pain is sharp, but then he uses his tongue to lick all around my folds before fucking me with his tongue.

I'm losing my mind.

I squirt, and cum gushes from me as I convulse and thrash. His tongue continues to go in and out while he pinches and alternately rubs my clit until my body shakes uncontrollably and my voice is hoarse. The orgasm is strong and violent, probably because he made me wait so long to have it. When I come down from my high, I register the sound of a condom packet ripping open before I feel his thick shaft push into me.

"Oh fuck," he says as he draws all the way out and slams back into me ever so slowly. He repeats the motion, even slower, and I'm so full and hot that I feel as though I will combust right on the table.

I call out his name, but he doesn't answer; he continues to work me over, slow stroke after slow stroke. I know if I don't do something soon, I might die from the need to cum. So, I lock my legs around his back and push him into me while I squeeze my pussy tight. It causes his concentration to stumble.

"Harder... faster..." I pant, and he obliges.

Never one to give up control for long, he pushes down on my stomach, pinning me to the cherry wood table. He leans his torso over to spread my thighs even wider while he slams into me with reckless abandon. I moan and shake my head from side to side as my walls clench.

"That's it, Lucia. Come for me, come for me right now."

And I do, my God, I do. There's no other choice as my screams echo through the house. Then he joins me with a shout and jerks inside of me. I feel the condom fill and the throbbing of his cock against my now relaxed walls.

He gives me a few last strokes before he collapses over me on the table. Our breathing is harsh as we try to catch our breath and slow our heart rates.

There's nothing left to say.

My husband fucked me into next week and I'm ready to do it again.

Rocco gets up first and unties my blindfold. He kisses each closed eye before slapping one of my breasts, which shakes me out of my sex-induced stupor.

"Let's go, dirty girl, you owe me a song. I'm in the mood for Verdi."

14

ROCCO

"Listen, you little Romano shit—if my daughter isn't released in the next twenty-four hours, I'll gut you like a pig and blow your entire fucking family into particles so small the vultures will choke on the dust."

Matteo Ricci's fury is all heat and hollow threats.

I spin in my leather chair, slow and lazy, letting my twenty-four-karat gold fidget spinner whir between my fingers. To him, I look like a man half-listening. In truth, I stopped hearing him completely about ten seconds ago.

Because in my head?

Lucia is playing *La donna è mobile.*

That goddamn aria—the one she drifted into on the piano after I'd laid her beautiful ass out on my dining table and fucked her senseless.

I asked her to play a song for me.

She snatched my goddamn soul.

She sat there, ass still red from my hand, fingers trembling as she coaxed that melody into the air like she was conjuring magic instead of notes.

I've been haunted by it ever since.

Every sensual flick of her wrist. Every swell of emotion in her face as she played Verdi like she *meant* it. Like she was translating everything I made her feel into music. Lust, defiance, surrender—woven into sound.

And now, while Ricci threatens war, all I can think about is how she looked—barefoot, wrecked, radiant—making music like it was her weapon and her offering all at once.

I should be buried between her thighs right now. I should be dragging her through a hike up the Path of the Gods, feeding her fresh figs and fucking her in a shepherd's cabin I had cleared out for the sole purpose of wrecking her soul.

Instead, I'm in Rome, babysitting a bastard who abandoned his daughter for twenty-four years and now has the nerve to pretend he's coming to save her.

He's too late.

Lucia belongs to me now.

She doesn't know where I am. I didn't leave a note. Didn't say goodbye.

She thinks I disappeared to clear my head.

What she doesn't know is I came here to remind her father—and the rest of the goddamn world—that she's no longer his to lose.

"She's not yours to take," I say flatly, finally cutting him off. "And she sure as fuck isn't yours to rescue."

Matteo lunges forward, slamming his fists on the desk between us. I don't flinch.

Four of his soldiers, packing concealed but heavy artillery, are at his back. I have the same protection. His soldiers are bigger, but mine are more vicious. I could cut the tension in the room with the Sebenza 25 blade strapped to my ankle. I know that one wrong move from any side will incite a bloodbath, so I must handle Matteo's anger and bruised ego with care.

After all, we're family now.

I exhale as he calls me one type of motherfucker after another. I regret that my current environment is a far cry from the comfort and peace of my coastal home.

That's why I don't have time for this shit. Matteo Ricci's rant has lasted five minutes too long, and I'm tired of the old man. He's so amped up that I haven't said a word, even though my patience wears thin.

Ricci is ruffled because he has no control over his situation, not because he's worried about Lucia.

He's a man known for his unwavering control, calm commands, and cool demeanor. Matteo Ricci orders a kill with the nod of his head.

His enemies often receive bullets with their names on them twenty-four hours before he kills them.

He's a monster who sat and enjoyed an entire Christmas meal, drinks included, with eight men he knew betrayed him without blinking an eye. When Matteo gave the last toast: *Alla salute*, which literally means to health, he immediately began to methodically kill every single man at the table with his infamous platinum handled AK-47, named *giustizia* or justice.

As the story goes, he cackled after the bloodshed, poured himself a drink, and muttered *to my continued health.*

His emotions rarely, if ever, come to the surface, and the most common way people describe him is that he is ice cold.

Tonight, I need to get him in line. We're in the office of my Rome penthouse in the center of Prati. It was built at the start of the 19th century, and it's one of the most affluent places in Rome. It's beautiful and the streets house some of my favorite luxuries, such as Brugnoli shoes. I may bring Lucia here one day if she's a good girl, but the truth is I'm rarely here. The home is more than just an essential real estate investment. It's perfect for a meeting like this.

The bastard hasn't taken one step towards Lucia in her entire life. Before the kidnapping of his daughter, he could pretend she wasn't valuable.

I knew better.

Men like Ricci and my uncle only care about two things: money and family. When Enzo discovered he had been placing money in her account since the day she was born, I knew I had Ricci by the balls. He always intended to collect on his investment. Beautiful women from our bloodlines can be bought for a hefty price and an invaluable alliance.

Now that he knows she could be in real danger, he's prepared to move heaven and earth.

Or kill me...

That's right where I want him.

If he kills me, he will have no way of getting to his daughter. Lucia and I've been in Amalfi for a little over a week, but I've scrambled every cell phone signal, and I've concealed my location from most maps. The only people who know my whereabouts are my pilot, my uncle, Enzo, and Mario. Ricci is up shit's creek, and he knows it.

That's why I don't mind waiting a few moments longer while he accepts the inevitability of his situation.

He slams a fist on my antique mahogany desk. I flick my eyes up to meet the fire in Matteo's, and my guards inch closer. I raise my hand to stop their encroachment and look my enemy in the eye.

"Well, don't you have anything to say to me, Romano?"

Finally!

"Yes. I want to begin by stating that my uncle and cousin are Romanos, and I serve as the former's consigliere. My father was Alberto Fieri, and I wear his name proudly.

A name that your daughter now shares as my wife, so you should learn to use it."

Silence and an unreadable mask fall over Ricci. He takes a moment to speak. Before he does, he slips into the seat in front of my desk. I nod to Mario, and he pours Matteo a glass of Macallan. He knocks the drink back in seconds and clears his throat.

"I never trusted your uncle, but I respected him. There's a code men live by. We don't fuck with each other's children. I hope he knows what he's done by taking my child and forcing her into his family, because there's no way in hell Lucia went willingly. She knows nothing about this life, and he will pay for dragging her into it. You will die a slow and painful death if any harm comes to her."

"Hmmm. Who says I want any harm to come to her? She's my wife and a beautiful woman. There are many more creative things I can do with her than kill her. Unlike the

Riccis, we're not in the habit of destroying beautiful things or killing innocent women."

The last words were a low blow, but I don't care. I know he ordered the murder of my mother and father, and according to the code, I should have killed him already.

I've wanted to so many times. Sometimes, at night, I find myself parked down the street from his home. I even snuck into his bedroom once, to watch him. The fucker sleeps like the dead.

His security is shit. Given enough time, Enzo can hack any system. When he looked at Matteo Ricci's system, he laughed and asked if I wanted the murder done in the next five minutes. The only reason he is alive is that I promised my uncle no more bloodshed. We've had peace for the past nineteen years, and I won't jeopardize the health of the family over my vendetta.

It's taken a considerable amount of self-awareness to refrain from projecting my hate of Matteo Ricci onto his daughter. She doesn't deserve it. Earlier, she tapped into my darker side by asking me to play for her. She has no idea that her father's machinations are why I stopped playing. I may be stern with her, but I'll never intentionally hurt her. There's no need.

However, I can fuck with her father's head. I'm sure he's imagining all the many ways I'm debauching his only daughter.

"What does Romano want? More territory? Money? Weapons. What's his price?" He hisses.

I laugh and drop my spinner on the desk in front of me. "Old man, you think you have all the answers, but you know nothing. My uncle has no malicious intent, and anything you can offer, he already has. Didn't you wonder why he would marry your daughter off to me and not his son? Wasn't that odd to you?"

"Nothing about you bloodsuckers surprises me. Cut the shit Fieri. Either prepare to die where you sit or give me my daughter back. I don't have time for riddles."

I scoff.

"Give her back? When did you ever have her? She's never even met you. In twenty-four years, not so much as a phone call from you. You're not exactly daddy dearest in her eyes. She hates you."

Ok, that's a stretch, but he doesn't know that.

"Fuck you."

He yells as he stands and pulls his gun. His mask has slipped again, but he quickly regains his composure. He continues with a softer tone that is tinged with regret, but he doesn't lower his weapon. He also doesn't flinch at the four now directly pointed at him.

"Don't you dare tell me anything about my relationship with my daughter. It wasn't my choice to stay out of her life; it was her mother's. She thought she would be safer that way. I thought so too, at first, but I quickly realized that was a mistake. I sent a letter every year on her birthday, asking to see her. But her mother never showed her any of them."

I contemplate his words quietly... and never take my eyes off the barrel of his gun.

He won't kill me. There's no advantage to that.

I don't buy his claim that he wanted a relationship with Lucia all along, but was stopped from pursuing it.

Men like us don't let many things get in our way. I've only known my wife for a short while, but it's clear she's vulnerable in this relationship. I will not allow him to hurt her to feed his possessiveness. In this thing of ours, we take what we want, whether it is things or people. There is no difference. And we don't take kindly to losing our possessions. He thinks I took something away from him. That's the real violation. This has nothing to do with love for his daughter.

"Ricci, I couldn't care less about your newly discovered parental instincts. I won't allow you to hurt Lucia with the false hope of a meaningful relationship with you. However, I care about what these instincts can do to help my family take down a thorn in both of our sides."

"Hmph," he huffs, lowers his gun, and drops back into his seat. "I'm glad we're back to business, Fieri. For a moment, I thought you cared about Lucia and her well-being. But it's just as I thought; you only care about leveraging her to support your family. Tell me, does she know how heartless you are? I bet you haven't even told her I came looking for her, since that doesn't serve your treacherous ends."

He's trying to get under my skin, but I won't let him. Lucia knows what type of monster she's married to, and she's slowly adjusting. She doesn't expect much from me emotionally, and I plan to keep it that way. But her father is a monster she doesn't know, and she doesn't deserve to be swallowed up in his world with no escape. She's too good for that.

"Ricci, before you insult me or my uncle any further, you

should know that it was my cousin Leo who attempted to kidnap Lucia to blackmail you. We caught wind of the idea and stopped him by getting to Lucia first. Leo wants to overthrow the Don and utilize the organization to initiate his violent ascent to power. He needs more manpower to accomplish that and would have used your soldiers to help him."

Ricci narrows his eyes. "What do you mean, my soldiers? I would lend none of my men to that snake and he knows it!" Matteo hisses.

I nod.

"Yes, he does. However, he also knows you might think differently about his proposition if Lucia were involved. If he truly had her, you might be easier to persuade. I only have your ear now, because I have something of value to you."

He takes a deep breath, and I watch as Mario pours more Macallan into his glass. After taking a deep gulp, he continues. "So, you usurped his plans and took Lucia instead. You're putting a price on Leo's head by telling me this. You want me to believe Romano would have his son killed? Why would he do that?"

"It's simple. My uncle is tired of cleaning up Leo's shit and, like you, he believes power and the Romano organization take precedence over his parental duties."

Ricci doesn't like my dig. I can tell by the way he's clenching his hand around his glass. It's too bad that I don't give a shit, so I continue.

"Our goal is to save Lucia from his clutches and bring you to our side instead of his.

Our two families need to join forces if we are going to beat Leo and his band of mercenaries without blood filling

Chicago's streets. Is that too hard to imagine? We also have powerful common enemies that would love to see our houses fall, such as the Russians and the Albanians. The last thing we need is to appear weak. That could fuel a war."

Ricci chuckles harshly. "Why do I need to join forces? What's in it for me and the Ricci family? The Romanos and the Riccis have coexisted for the last decade with no bloodshed, and it's suited me just fine. You stay on your side of the country, and I stay on mine. The Russians and the Albanians know if they fuck with the Ricci's, we'll erase their scum from the earth. We were left to run the drug racket while your family was granted our construction business and control of the unions. We've paid our penance to the Romano's and we've made a successful business. Now you want me to give you some of my men for a girl I barely know? So, some whore I fucked over 20 years ago said she was my daughter. A lot of women died trying to pin less on me. I let Chrisette live.

If you ask me, the last twenty-four years that Lucia has breathed are my gift to her."

My blood boils. His casual mention of penance for my parents' death makes me want to break his neck. I also don't like how he's talking about Lucia and her mother.

My glass slams on the desk and shatters as I rise from my seat. I keep my two hands on the desk and lean over to keep them from wrapping around his thick neck.

"You should care, fucker, because Leo isn't just coming for us, he's coming for every fucking family on the East Coast, including yours. You may not care about your daughter, but I know you care about the disgusting drug empire you've built. I don't buy your calm demeanor. You know both our organizations are vulnerable, which makes our families unsafe. It's crazy that you can't see that your daughter is worth three times any of this. If you weren't her father, I'd shove my pistol so far down your throat it would come out of your ass. Now you're with us or against us. If you don't want to help, I'll reach out to our West Coast allies. The great Matteo Ricci is only a myth if your daughter doesn't mean more to you than your pride.

His laugh comes quickly, as he claps his hands. He's genuinely amused.

"That was quite a demonstration, Fieri. You may have a heart beneath that stone chest after all. Since you seem to care so much about her, I will indulge you. But I don't have to explain my life to you. I did the best I could, so yes, I sent her money. Even if Chrisette wouldn't take it, she knew it was there. There's security in knowing there's a net in case you fall. Financial security is the foundation of success. I guess your father didn't teach you that one. So she could pretend I had nothing to do with Lucia being one of the finest concert pianists in the world, but I know I did. Or at least my money did. I won't let you destroy what I've built. I know you haven't told her about me; if I were in your place, I would do the same. I'd make myself the center of her world. But I'm letting you know right now when that fucker Leo is done, I'm coming for her, and you won't stop me. She's my daughter; la mia carne e il mio sangue.

I hiss my following words with deadly precision. "She may be your flesh and blood, but she's my wife, and she's mine. Don't think for one second you can get her away from me.

I'll kill you first. If you fuck us over, I'll make sure you never see her or the light of day again."

"What about what Lucia wants?"

I scoff.

"What Lucia wants is inconsequential. She knows her place. She's a Romano now, and her life will be in service to this family, not her father's. Her sacrifice will usher in one of the greatest mafia alliances in the last fifty years. Once we have an heir, he will cement our ties in blood. We will be unstoppable."

"You have balls Fieri, I'll give you that. You've taken my daughter, demanded my cooperation and use of my men, and told me to go fuck myself in more than one way today. You should die a very slow and painful death for your disrespect."

"I welcome you to try, but I must warn you. It's not an easy win."

He leans over the desk towards me with clenched fists firmly planted on top of the beautiful wood. "Time will tell how easy it is to kill you, Fieri. In the meantime, what's the rest of your brilliant plan?"

I rock back into my seat.

"My next move is to go home to my wife and fuck her brains out. However, my capo Mario will stay with you to discuss our next move."

Ricci exhales and leans back into his chair. He's an old man who's been in the game too long. Suddenly, he stands and grabs my arm from across the desk. I hear guns cock all around and for a moment I wonder if I overplayed my hand.

"You better not lose one hair on her head, Fieri. She's all I got. I'll cut your balls off and shove them down your throat if any harm comes to her. I need assurance that she's safe."

"All I have to give you is my word. She's never been safer than the moment she became my wife."

"Keep it that way, or they won't be able to find a trace of you when I'm done."

With that, he walks out.

I may have to kill that bastard after all.

15

LUCIA

Something shifted in me the night Rocco Fieri devoured my soul on his antique dining room table.

And by soul, I mean my pussy.

God help me, just remembering it makes my thighs clench and my cheeks burn.

He didn't just go down on me—he worshipped me. Like a man kneeling at the altar of sin, and I was the only god worth believing in.

He ate like he was starving.

Like every moan from my lips was a prayer, he needed to survive.

The only other thing I've seen him attack with that kind of hunger?

His secret stash of chocolate cannolis.

Yeah. I know about those.

He thinks he's slick—sneaking off to his office at

midnight like I won't notice Mr. Discipline stuffing his face with pastry and sweetened ricotta like it's a holy ritual.

But I see everything.

I should feel guilty for spying.

I don't.

This man has stripped me of every ounce of privacy I've ever known—down to my fucking panties and my sense of autonomy. The least I'm owed is the satisfaction of knowing he has a weakness that comes wrapped in pastry and shame.

It makes him human. Almost.

Maybe that's why he works out like a possessed demon every morning at 5 a.m.—to punish his body for the indulgences he pretends don't exist. He thinks I'm asleep when he slips out of bed, but I'm not. I hear the soft creak of the mattress, the tension in his breath, the way he paces before pulling on a shirt like he's already fighting something I can't see.

He's restless. Coiled too tight.

Whatever made Rocco Fieri into the man he is—the calculating monster who dragged me into this world and claimed me as his—still follows him into the night.

And yet...

Somewhere in the last few days, something in him changed, too.

He's still hard. Still ruthless. Still obsessed with owning me like I'm a prized violin he plays only when the world is on fire. But now, there's a strange tenderness hiding beneath the steel. A quiet consideration. He asks if I'm cold. He brushes my hair off my shoulder before I fall asleep. He brings me books I never asked for and pretends it's nothing.

He doesn't smile—but he sees me now.

And that, somehow, is even more dangerous than his belt or his bullets.

Because the more he acts like I matter, the more I start to wonder what it would feel like to be his *wife* in every way that counts.

And that is the start of madness.

"Mrs. Fieri, may I come in?"

The knock at my door, alongside Maria's welcoming voice, coaxes me out of bed for the day. I'm still surprised whenever she refers to me as Mrs. Fieri. I'm Rocco's wife, but doesn't she know that it's all a sham?

When he first introduced us, the day after I arrived, Maria was overjoyed and extremely excited to tell me that Mr. Fieri had never had any women here.

Like I should feel special I was chosen to be tied to a monster in every way conceivable because my father doesn't give a damn.

Any dreams I had of her being the sweet old lady who would help me escape were dashed the moment I was met with her enthusiastic welcome. No one in this house goes against Rocco's wishes. *No one.*

"Yes, Maria. I'm up. You may come in."

She waltzes in carrying two Lululemon shopping bags and a polite smile. The seventy-year-old woman moves with the grace of a swan and the speed of a woman half her age. Every day, she wears her uniform: a sleek black wrap dress with black Louboutin heels. Her silver hair stays pinned in a perfect Chignon, and she runs this house with an iron fist. She's the ultimate warm demander. Where Rocco rules through fear and intimidation, she maintains the staff's discipline through mutual respect and high expectations.

"I'm happy to see you looking so energetic this morning. Mr. Rocco has asked that you wear these things for your hike today. I hope they are to your liking."

I guess this means my husband has returned from wherever he's been the past few days. *The bastard.* I was hiding from him because whenever he's close my body acts like a two dollar whore. But I liked knowing he was there. He makes me feel safe. When he left, I felt exposed and empty.

On the other hand, I've begged to get out of this lovely prison he calls his home. I'm not excited about a hike, but as long as I'm out of this pretty prison. I'm happy. *He listened.*

Walking over to her, I kiss her cheek hello, and take the two bags from her. " I'm sure I will love whatever you've picked for me, Maria. I always do."

"Me!" she scoffs and breaks into a bit of laughter before snatching the bags back to walk over to my bed to methodically lay out each piece of athleisure.

"I do not pick out your clothes, Mrs. Fieri. Mr. Rocco does, and with great care."

My eyes pop open. "Rocco picks out my clothes!"

I don't know why that knowledge matters to me or why the idea of me wearing something he chose makes me shiver. I knew he was bossy, and I figured that his telling me what to wear was an extension of his domineering nature. Knowing that he takes time to pick out each garment himself makes me feel foolish. Suddenly, I am frustratingly eager to please him.

"Yes, of course he does. Mr. Fieri takes great care with

any and all decisions pertaining to your health and well-being."

I look for hidden meaning behind Maria's words, but there isn't any. She's talking like what she says is straight facts and nothing more or less.

"If that's all, Mrs. Fieri, I will go and get started with the rest of my day. I will send breakfast up soon. If you need anything else in the meantime, just let me know."

After I nod and smile, Maria waves goodbye, and I'm left behind with my handpicked costume for the day.

When he disappeared for a few days, I had no idea where he went. It's not like I could call him since I still don't have a phone at my disposal. I didn't want to care that he left me here alone, but I did. I spent the two days reading and moping around like I'd lost my best friend until I snapped myself out of it. For all I know, the man was fucking the woman he really loves and leaving me to stew under the watchful eyes of my babysitters-the bodyguards.

I'm relieved now that I know he's back. But if I don't keep a simmering hatred for my husband, I may fall for him, and that won't do. Before he left, he promised me he would take me outside, just to get me out of the house. Now he tells me it's a hike.

I'm not sure whether I should be excited or scared.

Before my kidnapping, I counted walking half a mile from my apartment to campus as exercise, but I'm not in the appropriate physical shape for a hike. But against my better judgment, I'm going because I'm excited to experience the Italian coastline with Rocco. He knows everything about the Amalfi Coast, and through listening to the servants, I learned that he cares deeply about the land. He subsidizes approximately fifty lemon groves across the region to keep them profitable. Amalfi's younger generation has no desire to keep the massive farms running, and the older generation needs help. Rocco doesn't want the old ways of farming to die, so he keeps the groves running.

Shit like this keeps me confused about how I feel about him.

No matter how noble his local efforts, I can't forget to keep my wits about me. This is not the man to fawn over or fall in love with. I'm mad I let my body betray me a few nights ago after dinner.

I never should have fucked him.

It was deliciously good but wrong.

So, so, wrong!

Rocco Fieri is my kidnapper or, at most, a reluctant bodyguard. Husband be damned; if it weren't for my father's blood running through my veins Rocco Fieri wouldn't take two looks at me. I'm convinced of that.

I know nothing of his past or the women he's been with before, but I can guess his type. Model thin, flawless skin, shiny hair, and unparalleled beauty. All the things I am not. It's clear from his wardrobe and home that he has a distinct aesthetic. He values beautiful things. If how he treats me is any indication, women are simply beautiful things he collects.

Rocco Fieri doesn't take no for an answer, and the power exuding off him is even sexier than his rock-hard abs, Grecian profile, and strokable hair. *Women like power.* I have no doubt that Alesandro catches more pussy than Seby Zavala in my beloved Comiskey Park.

My marriage is one of convenience, and I'd do well to remember that. Sometimes, I wish he wouldn't be nice at all because it's too confusing. Other times, I'm grateful for the reprieve.

I'm not the kind of woman men chase. I am the woman that men overlook. I'm pretty enough, but I've always been a nerd. I like classical literature. I collect vintage jewelry and converse with older people about their past experiences. History fascinates me, and the future scares me. I'll take a good New York-style pizza over a lobster dinner any day. I'm proud of my hair, but the maintenance of it doesn't consume me. Makeup is only a necessity of performance life, and I can't remember the last time I went shopping on purpose. Point being, I'm not your typical woman, and most men don't know how to approach me. So, they don't.

Before I was kidnapped, I was comfortable in my obscurity. I never had to fend off unwanted advances or figure out how to deal with the ones who wanted me. The opposite sex is a mystery. The only reason I allowed my college boyfriend to take my virginity was to get the ritual over with. Now, for reasons I'll never understand, I have a husband who's a walking sexual innuendo, and I'm out of my depth.

He demands all of me, but I can't trust him. I feel like holding back this one thing is keeping him in check. I know it's wild. He's already fucked me and the man could take it anytime he wants. But, he told me he wouldn't, and I believe him. That makes me respect him just a little.

I skim over the price tags of everything laid out for me and soft gag. The amount of money the man spends on clothing is ludicrous.

After tying the laces of the $800 hiking boots Maria laid out for me, I'm ready for my first date with my husband. I walk over to the mirror and glance at the Lululemon workout pants, matching sports bra, and jacket. Everything is brand new, and the tags were still attached before I put the items on. This entire outfit costs more than $ 1,500. The way he throws money away is shocking, but I do like knowing he prepared these things just for me.

When I make it downstairs, I'm happy to see that his back is to me as he whispers harshly with Mario about something. It gives me a few minutes to appreciate him in all his glory. His ass looks especially delicious in the workout pants he's wearing. I never knew close-fitting dri-fit fabric could look so good on a man.

Sensing my presence, he turns around and catches me salivating like a creeper. The right side of this mouth lifts in a smirk; *he's so full of himself.* I'm not helping to deflate his ego by staring at him like some lunatic.

"Sorry to interrupt, but are we ready to go?"

Rocco throws me a quick smile and gestures for me to head outside before turning back to Enzo and Mario. It seems he needs to finish that conversation before we go anywhere, and he doesn't want me to hear it.

That pisses me off.

Ever since we got here, Rocco has been on edge. He's always sneaking off with those two to meet and whisper in corners of the house. Seeing as those clandestine meet-and-greets likely concern me, their sneaking around makes me anxious and leaves me in the dark. No one tells me anything.

Rocco treats me like a child, Mario treats me with

disdain, while Enzo ignores my very existence. The most I've gotten out of him is a grunt.

From my observations, Enzo is the quietest member of their group. I overheard the servants refer to him as a tech genius. He's over surveillance and security. If something has a passcode, he can hack it. Enzo is sharp and ruthless, looking like a sexy Clark Kent wannabe with his thick, dark curls, chiseled jaw, Prada frames, and tall frame. His hazel eyes blaze with a fiery orange and dance with a never-ending curiosity.

He's got an aura of wildness that floats off him, and it's clear that he's the most unpredictable. I imagine he has oceans of blood on his hands. I have no doubt that he knows what's really going on and could get me in contact with my father. But that's never going to happen if Enzo won't even acknowledge me, let alone talk.

All I know is that whatever made Rocco leave our bed on such short notice must be essential, and I wonder if it has anything to do with Leo or my father.

If it were the latter, I think I would know. After all, I'm being used as leverage to secure an alliance with him. If they had contact with him, I'm sure I would know by now. Rocco promised he would let me know the moment my father makes any positive contact. He's many things, but he doesn't strike me as a man who breaks his promises.

That leads me to believe it's Leo causing the turmoil. Which makes me think about my safety and how vulnerable my position is. I just wish we could find my father already and plan our attack on Leo. The sooner I'm out from under

Rocco's thumb, the sooner I can try to negotiate parts of my life back.

I track Rocco's movements through the door windows. When he dismisses Mario and Enzo, he walks out and plants a kiss on my forehead.

"Sorry to keep you waiting, Lucia. We have a forty-five-minute drive from Ravello to the starting point of our hike, a little hamlet named Bomerano. We'll end in Positano, where we have reservations for dinner."

I arch my eyebrows in surprise. "You expect me to be dinner-ready after a hike? I'll be a sweaty mess and not dressed for any of the ritzy restaurants I'm sure you frequent."

He laughs. "You should know by now that I plan for every inevitability. I have already secured a suite for us at my favorite hotel, Le Sirenuse. We will make a pit stop there before we head to dinner."

When I land on the bottom step, Rocco twirls a curl of my hair in his fingers while he leans in close. "Then I can have dessert before dinner in our hillside, sea-view suite. As you already know, you are my favorite meal accompaniment."

I swallow, knowing I'm likely a blushing mess. Why does he always have to talk so dirty? It keeps me hot, bothered, and confused. Now all I can think about is that skillful tongue of his licking my pussy with expert stroke.

Clearing my throat, I attempt to change the subject. "Exactly how long will this hike take us? I'm not exactly in athletic shape, you know?"

I graze over his athletic form and inwardly grimace at my

lack of discipline. I've never had body issues, but I'm not a little girl. I have ass and hips for days. Whenever Rocco returns from a workout shirtless, or strips before entering our bed at night I suck my stomach in a bit tighter wondering if my body appeals to him. I can't help but think that this is all about convenience, rather than actual desire. He would never approach me on the streets of Chicago for a date of any kind.

Sensing my unease with his usual keenness, he places his finger beneath my chin and tilts my head up into his gaze. "Soon, I will know your body better than you do. I already know how to make you come on my fingers and tongue with minimal effort. You are a goddess, and your body is a temple that I plan to worship often. You need to own it, push it, and love it. I never want you to compare yourself to me or anyone else. I want you to be comfortable in the skin you're in. That starts with this hike. It will push you, but you'll be better for it."

How does he do that? How does he peel back all my layers and tear down all the walls I erect to keep myself safe from not just him, but the world? This marriage is a fucking disaster, but I'm determined to make it out alive and return to my life, my music, and my goals. I know I'll never play the piano professionally again if I fall for Rocco and lose my will to escape from him, my father, and everything the mafia traps you with. Shaking off his touch, I look him square in the eye.

"All that may be true, but how long is this hike going to take? I'd like to mentally prepare. I like the outdoors, but only at my own pace."

He chuckles, "At the pace we're tackling the mountain, la

mia piccola palla di fuoco, it should only take us approximately three hours, give or take a few minutes. However, since we'll be making pit stops along the way, we'll be out on the mountain for a total of five or six hours. We will be in our suite by seven. Dinner reservations are at nine."

With his hand at the small of my back, I nod and allow him to push me towards the waiting SUV.

"Now, we need to be on our way. I don't want to lose any more sunlight."

I don't want to lose anymore of myself.

16

ROCCO

Baby girl is tired.

I may have underestimated the complexity of this hike and overestimated her ability to complete it. The thing is, it's not her body holding her back. I know she thinks it is. She's hard on herself and I fucking hate it. Her body is beautiful and full of curves that I obsess over. However, since she's not a model's size, society has her doubting herself, and that doubt is what's causing this hike to take almost twice as long as it should.

She thinks she's going to fall.

It's her anxiety causing her to stumble.

She's nervous about every step she takes, and that causes a double-take at every motion forward. Upon taking a look around, I can see that this hike is not for beginners. There is little to no railing to protect you from the sea thousands of feet below you. The trail is not as polished as I remember. The last mile has been rocky and unblemished mountain terrain. She's anxious and her fear exasperates me.

As if I would ever let anything happen to her. *She's mine.*

I won't even let Mother Nature have her. The crazy thing is, I no longer have a clear picture of why she's mine or what she's here for. I've got her father by his balls. Mario informed me that their follow-up meeting went on without a hitch. There's a plan to take out Leo through a fake drug exchange with Ricci.

Leo still thinks that Ricci is on his side and will supply him with the first shipment of drugs he needs to break into his line of business. Ricci is only charging him 25% of the profits in perpetuity since he's getting to sell on our turf. The deal also includes him lending Leo some soldiers when he assassinates our don, his father.

Leo knows that there will be a bloody war after he takes out his father, and he needs Ricci's support. But he will never get that far. When he goes to the docks to meet Ricci's capo Enrico, he will instead meet Enzo, Mario, and the barrel of my gun. It should all be wrapped up within a week.

Today, it is all about endearing Lucia to me even more. I need her thoroughly fucked and high off my cock before all this goes down. I want her emotionally tied to me so her loyalty is with me and not her father after the smoke clears.

Technically, she's still in a lot of danger until Leo is dead, and no one will keep her safer than I will. I don't quite trust Ricci to do right by her.

Enzo discovered some suspicious deposits in Leo's bank accounts. It makes sense to see one or maybe two transactions from Ricci to him. After all, the sham drug deal takes some capital. But Enzo found deposits that date back over a year. The depositor is a shell company owned by none other than Matteo's capo, Enrico Manetti.

What could he possibly be paying Leo for in the tune of two million dollars? Does Matteo even know?

Something is off.

Other than my paranoia, I have no real reason to keep her from her father. I could arrange a meeting, or at least let her know I've met with him. But I won't. I need her to be dependent on me for just a bit longer.

I'm a selfish bastard. I want her to feel as crazy and off balance about me as I do about her.

I try not to think about how arousing her smell is. When I sneak out of my bed early to leave her, I sniff her hair to get a hit. I refuse to acknowledge how I look forward to our dinners at home. Seeing her in my element, in my favorite place on earth, does things to my chest I don't recognize. She belongs here, and I like it this way. The campaign to make her want to be mine starts now. She won't leave this mountain the same way she arrived.

"Rocco, I hate this. Why did you make me hike this stupid mountain? I could die out here with any step I take. Why isn't there any railing? Is this a public trail? I've only seen one other pair of hikers. Do you plan on abandoning me out here or something?"

I'm trying not to laugh at her feisty stance. She's sweaty and tired but still has enough fire to place her hands on her hips and give me a piece of her mind. Her hair has flown from under her carefully tied silk scarf and sweatband, and I can tell she's just over it at this point. I don't laugh because I know it will only anger her further, so instead I give her the most serious face I can muster as I close the distance between us.

"No, my Lucia. I would never leave you. We only have about a quarter of a smile to go before we get to your surprise. Just be patient.

"Yeah, Ok," she huffs. "You've promised me some big reveal for the past two miles, and all I see is more of this stupid mountain. My body aches, and I'm sure my hair looks like a bird's nest at this point. I don't like being afraid to fall every minute of this hike, and it's also a bit warm. I'm sweating like a man, and no part of this is enjoyable. I hate to sound like a complaining brat, but that's where I am at the moment."

I don't reply. Instead, I turn around and keep trekking down the mountain. Engaging her while she's in this mood will do me no good.

We continue in silence for about thirty minutes until she catches a glimpse of twinkling lights ahead.

"What's that!" she gasps. " I hope it's somewhere to sit down!

I snicker. " It's even better than that, Lucia. It's somewhere to lie down."

I feel her hand on my shoulder, and she slips a bit, trying to gain her footing. " I don't sleep outside Fieri!"

She shouldn't make sudden movements when she's this close to the mountain's edge, especially since she's scared of heights. I grasp her hand from behind to steady her. She turns and grabs me onto me for dear life. The bear hug takes me by surprise, but her trust pleases me.

"Be careful, piccola ragazza," I whisper. "I can't have you falling to your death."

She nuzzles into my shirt more. "You always save me. Why? Why do you care at all?"

I have no answer that I'm prepared to give. I can't tell her that she's become my air; the real reason I wake every morning. I haven't earned the right to imprint upon her heart that way, and I'm not even sure I can hold up my end of a love bargain. It's better if she's left in the dark; that way her heart won't get involved.

I bite down gently on her shoulder and raise my eyes to mine. "You know why piccola ragazza. What is the only reason a man like me would keep a woman like you alive and breathing? Why won't I let anything hurt one hair on your head?"

She huffs. "Because if I'm hurt, then you can't use me as a pawn in your little mafia games. You want me to stay alive long enough for that, right?" She shoves away from me, careful of

Her venom irks my nerves. I don't want her to fall for me, but she can show some respect. I know she's uncomfortable, but she also has front seats for one of the most sought-after views in the world. If she got out of her head, she would realize that. Getting her out of her thoughts is precisely what I'm here for.

"No, I want you to live long enough for me to properly fuck you. That tryst on my dining room table was just an appetizer."

I don't miss her sharp intake of breath. That sound is

blood to a shark like me. In time, I will reroute her energy to better use.

I smooth the back of my hand down her jaw and neck. "I am determined to fill every hole you have with my dick Lucia. You will be completely mine in every physical way possible. You will scream my name in pleasure and have no doubt of who owns this beautiful body before you see your maker. Don't even think about dying before I get my hands on you."

I wrap my hand around the nape of her neck and pull her in for a hard kiss. She doesn't resist me; instead, the little vixen grinds her body against mine. My words made her hot. My Lucia doesn't need poetry and flowers. The cold hard truth paired with a hot hard cock turns her on. I'm more than happy to oblige.

When I release her, she stabs me with a glare. "You're an asshole Fieri." She walks ahead of me towards the twinkling lights, and I rub my bottom lip, laughing. She's mad that she wants me. I can't be blamed for that. Her body wants what it wants. It should be addressed to me, her husband.

When she gets to the mouth of the cave that holds the shepherd's house, her entire body reacts. The space has been completely transformed into a five-star glamping experience. I have colorful Turkish carpets laid across the stone floors and at least 100 cream and gold pillows strewn around.

In the center of the rug, there's an ice bucket with Dom Perignon and those silly Izze drinks she likes-apple flavor only, along with an extensive charcuterie board. Café lights illuminate the space, and soft music plays from the Bluetooth speakers my team left for us. I made a playlist of her favorite love songs. Sure, I hacked into her phone to find out what they were, but I think the end justifies the means.

"This is an exquisite space, Rocco." Seeing her face light up tells me I made the right decision. " Oh my gosh! I love this song!"

Aretha Franklin belts out the words to "Call Me," and I smile. In my line of work, this is a song Lucia may hum to herself quite often. When your husband is consigliere to one of the biggest mafia outfits in the country, you tend to want him to call the moment he gets wherever he's going. But will she ever call me her "dearest of all," or declare "I love you?" Do I even want that?

I take her hand and lead her inside the cave. "Come and rest your feet. You can sit or lie anywhere you like."

She bites her bottom lip and throws me a shy smile. "OK, are you joining me?"

I nod. " Of course. With you here, where else would I go?"

She shrugs and drops her crossbody bag and water bottle on the rug before flopping her sexy body down. I look down at her and feel ravenous. Lucia is the curviest woman I've ever had the pleasure of touching. Her full breasts, narrow waist, and full hips make me want to slam into her until she begs for mercy. She was made to be pleased with a firm hand and soft touch. Right now, I could lick every inch of her toasted almond skin and then eat her alive.

Patience.

I sit against pillows on a rock opposite her and gesture for her to stretch her legs. "Bring your feet to my lap, piccola ragazza. You've complained the last four miles about how much your feet hurt. Let me make it up to you."

She gives me a wary look. " Rocco, my feet are sweaty, and they may stink at this point. It will repulse you." She laughs.

I shake my head. " I don't care about sweat. You could never repulse me, Lucia. I'm obsessed with every inch of you in any state. Now don't make me ask you again. Give me your feet."

She obeys, and I gently remove her shoes and socks before getting to work. I start with her heels to ease the pain. She moans in relief, and that only makes me want her to moan in true pleasure at my hands. Reflexology raises arousal, so I target points on the bottom of her feet that bring joy. One foot at a time, I carry her to the point of bliss.

"My God, you're good at that, Rocco." She closes her eyes and lays her head back on the pillow behind her.

I smirk. " I'm good at a great many things, Lucia. Remember how I made the rest of your body feel? You will get that and even more tonight if you just let go.

Her right eye pops open. "You brought me here to fuck me didn't you? How much is this foot rub going to cost me?"

I don't flinch. "Everything."

I zero in on the pulse point at the base of her throat and observe her increased breathing. She's either nervous or horny. Maybe a bit of both. Either way, I can't give her too much time to think herself out of this. Tonight is the night. Not only do I need to cement our marriage further before her father gets in her ear, but I need her like I've never needed another woman before. I can't wait another minute to get inside her.

When I finish her foot rub, I pull my jacket and T-shirt over my head. My eyes never leave hers, and I pin her to the ground. She receives the message and quickly removes her pullover. She hesitates with her shirt, but once she gets her courage, she moves quickly. The black sports bra I bought her is as sexy on her as a $500 piece of lace from La Perla.

I pour her a glass of the Dom, and while she sips from her glass, I take a swig from the bottle.

She giggles. "Animal."

I wink and drink another swig before refilling her glass. A nice buzz will do her well tonight. Once she's finished that glass, I pour her another half a glass and finish the bottle off myself.

When I stand, her eyes follow my every move. First, I remove my shoes and socks. Then, I drop my pants and boxer briefs in one swift movement. My semi-hard cock salutes her and she responds by licking her lips, never taking her eyes off my manhood. The attention only makes me harder, and I know I need to feel her warm mouth on me.

I reach down and pull her by her hands to her knees. Leaning over, I unsnap her sports bra by flicking the front latch. *Thank God for front-hooking bras.* When I stand back up, the tip of my cock brushes her lips and I swear I hear her moan. The touch makes me hiss, and I know if I don't take care, I'll blow my load way too early tonight.

"I want you to suck my dick Lucia. Do you want me to fill that pretty mouth of yours with my cum?"

Her dilated eyes tell me all I need to know, but I appreciate the nod all the same. "I can't be gentle," I warn her.

"I don't expect you to be. Just don't expect me to be gentle either."

Well fuck me...

"Take care piccola ragazza. That mouth may write a check your throat can't cash. Open wide for me, I won't wait any longer."

Slowly I feed her my dick until I feel the back of her throat and hear the sexiest gagging sound on earth. Once I know she can take me, I slip out, and she drags her tongue against my length.

"Fuck," I hiss. Then I wrap my hand in her ponytail and pull her mouth back onto my dick. I thrust and jam my throbbing cock back down her throat and try not to cum like a sixteen year-old.

This woman may be the death of me.

17

LUCIA

I take every inch of his cock as he freely feeds my throat.

I don't know what's gotten into me, but power radiates throughout my body while I swallow him whole.

Rocco warned me he wasn't gentle, and he didn't lie. When he pulls out of my mouth again, I catch my breath, but he rams right back down my throat with no mercy.

He's fucking my mouth like it's a pussy and that makes me want to touch mine.

Desperately I spread my knees further apart and dip my hands into my underwear to find my clit. Rubbing furiously, I get wet enough to stick two fingers inside my damp heat while I moan onto his cock.

"Yes, my dirty little girl. Are you fucking yourself, while I fuck this mouth of yours? Does my cock sliding down your tight throat make you want to touch yourself?"

He tightens his grip on my hair and keeps control of the

pace. But I can tell from the hitch in his voice that he's coming soon. Knowing that I'm the one making this powerful man lose control is the biggest turn-on of all.

His pace picks up, and I know he won't last much longer. I pick up the pace between my legs, and he growls when he sees me working.

"I'm going to cum and fill your pretty little mouth and you will swallow every drop," he growls like a wild animal.. " If you miss one drop I'll spank your ass red. Do you understand?"

I choke and then moan at the visual of his strong hands across my ass. The image is too much, and I cry from the pleasure coursing through me. I'm ready to blow when he yanks my hair with a hard tug and pulls me off his dick. Then he says two words that destroy me.

"Don't Come!"

Fuck. I'm crazy with need, but obeying him makes me even hotter.

Or Crazier.

Before I can cry over my unspilled milk, it flows down my throat.

"Fuck Lucia, Fuuuuucccccckkkk." he roars and empties all he has inside of me.

I swallow every ounce of his essence and suck his cock hard to pull every drop of cum he has like his good girl. When I'm done, I look up at his sweaty panting face and internally pat myself on the back. His eyes are wild with lust, and his words are hoarse and unsteady. *I did that to him.*

"Get on your back!" he barks in a harsh whisper. I shiver at the command and follow his orders without a moment's hesitation. I reach down to discard my pants and under-wear, but he slaps my hand away.

"Did I ask you to do that? Do only what I task you with, and you will be rewarded. Now place your hands over your head and lift your hips."

I obey and am rewarded with a fiery kiss while he takes his time stripping me naked. When he comes up for air, he nips and pinches at each of my nipples before lavishing each with a soft caress using the tip of his tongue.

"Open your legs!" He commands.

I spread my thighs for him, but apparently, not wide enough. He slaps both of my thighs, demanding that I go wider. When I'm done, my body is open and bare for him. I'm presented like a pig for slaughter. My hands are above my head, which makes my breasts sit up higher, and my nipples are rock hard. My pussy is on display, and while that would generally make me red in the face; right now, all I can do is lick my lips and anticipate whether his tongue or dick will cover her soon.

He doesn't make me wait long to find out. With an open mouth kiss, he devours my clit to bring me hot and high. I scream his name loud enough that any shepherds lingering around to gather their goats and sheep on this mountain are getting an earful. I was so worked up from the blow job that it doesn't take long for me to squirt out my pleasure once he adds two fingers to press inside me.

"That's it piccola ragazza, that's it baby, come for me," he murmurs against my pussy.

I squirt, cream, and moan until I'm nothing more than a weightless orgasm, seeing stars in a dark cave. When I finally come down and the bursts of color fade from behind my eyes; I look up and stare into his artic blue eyes as he quickly sheaths on a condom before slowly pressing his dick inside my tight opening. His hands hold my thighs wide, and I'm at his mercy.

The stretch is a painful pleasure I've dreamt about since he last took me. Before him, I'd only been touched here once, and it was nothing like this. I brace for his next inch, and my keening betrays just how much I want him as well as just how much it hurts.

His hand reaches for my cheek, and he holds me there. "Yes, Lucia. Take all of me. I'm right here with you. Are you ready, baby girl? Are you ready to become completely mine? There's no turning back."

I nod and beg for his cock to continue to press into me. I need him. I need him to fill me and remind me that the world of mobsters and killers doesn't matter because he is with me, and I am his. He will never let anything happen to me, and together we can take the world by storm.

"Fuck!" He roars as he pushes the last six or so inches inside me. The burn takes my breath away. "Breathe, Lucia, breathe!"

He slaps my right breast, and a loud breath expels from my mouth. He leans down to kiss me senseless and his tongue ends up on the side of my neck biting and licking as he starts a slow groove that makes my pussy melt.

The pleasure is undeniable; it's like nothing I've ever felt before. I grab onto his ass and hold tight as he works my body over like a precious piece of machinery that only he knows how to work.

"That's it, baby, open for me. Take it all."

When I do, he picks up his pace to fuck me like the hounds of hell are nipping at his heels. He moves like his salvation is on the other side of my pussy and he's ready to be set free from whatever holds him hostage.

"Mine. You're mine." He growls, and I close my eyes to let the orgasm wash over me like a baptism by fire. I come again for the second time, and the world stops for me. He slaps my thighs to bring me back to reality, and I scream.

"That's it, baby girl. Let the hills hear you cum for me again."

"I can't," I cry. "I can't." I shake my head and plead for pity, but he only presses harder.

"Yes, you can and you will!" He picks up both of my legs and throws them over his left shoulder, while continuing to thrust himself into me at a furious pace. Rocco fucks me until I see the moon, stars, mountains, and rivers. I swear I see heaven, and that's when I know that my life has officially turned into a top 20 R&B song. But who cares? If this is what sex with Rocco is like, I'll be that and more.

When I cry my release, my body shakes and my pussy clamps down around his dick, placing it in a chokehold. With a shout, he joins my pleasure and comes inside me. While he releases, he leans over to bite my neck until there's nothing left besides the air we breathe.

When he catches his breath, he lands a soft kiss on my forehead, but he doesn't pull out of me. He turns to his side and takes me with him so that we're facing each other but still connected. I feel our mingled juices run down my thigh.

He ripped me apart and put me back together again. *I am new.*

The sticky evidence of our lovemaking doesn't disgust me, it delights me. He hugs me tight and I recognize that we are fucked up; but damnit we are one.

Whether we live or die, we'll be together.

18

ROCCO

Mornings are different now.

Before I married Lucia, I woke up every morning at 6:00 a.m. sharp to complete a daily 90-minute High-Impact Training workout.

Then I would shower and meet Maria in the kitchen for breakfast, which consisted of three hard-boiled eggs, fresh olive oil, and thinly sliced prosciutto, served with toast.

If I were in Chicago, Mario and Enzo would stop by to brief me on my schedule for the day and detail any clean-up from their crews' work from the night before. If I were anywhere else in the world, they would FaceTime me. Either way, by 9:00 am, I was out of the house and heading to various meetings to start my 12-hour day.

It is now 9:02 am and I am between the legs of Lucia licking her pussy awake. My wife is a powerful distraction. Her sweet side must be earned, and since we returned from our mountain hike a month ago, I've been obsessed with bringing it out. My campaign starts every morning with oral sex, breakfast in bed, and a thorough fucking before I run off to rule the world.

"Mmmm, that feels good."

I lift my head to look at her, but she pushes my head back down. "No, don't stop. Please."

I smile against her cunt and dive back into my breakfast. She'll come twice on my tongue before she gets to eat the strawberry waffles she loves so much. I swear, if I don't stop indulging her, we'll both be too large to fit through the door. But it's impossible to say no to her over small things when I know I can never give her the things she really wants.

She desires independence and a career as a classical pianist. Instead, she's married to the mafia and the daughter of one of the most dangerous men in America. Life's not always fair, but I think I can manage to bring a bit of joy into her life.

I long to protect her from worry and danger. Right now, all I can do is overwhelm her with pleasure and spoil her rotten. Enzo lost track of Leo, and we have no idea where he is. He hasn't reached out, and his silence is ominous.

What is that little fucker up to?

"Ahhh Ahhh Rocco..." Lucia moans and pushes my head further into her sweet honey. Her taste makes me forget all about Leo and his treachery. After she trembles and climaxes, she releases me from the sweet prison between her legs.

I'm preparing for round two when I'm interrupted by a knock at the door.

'What!" I yell. Whoever is on the other end of the door has a death wish.

"Uncle Roc, it's me!" A cute four-year-old voice calls out, and my heart clenches.

Lucia giggles, and I wink as I slap her thigh. "Come on, get dressed."

My Aria is here. I know Enzo is using her as a decoy. He knows not to disturb me in the mornings. The early hours belong to my sexy wife, but I can't bash his head in front of his daughter and my godchild. *Smart Man.*

He disappeared on me two days ago to fly to Chicago unexpectedly. I was told not to worry and to enjoy my wife; so if he's here, shit must be bad.

"Do I finally get to meet the infamous Aria? Enzo hides her from me as if I were a leper."

I barely register what she's saying because I'm mesmerized by the show taking place in front of me. Watching Lucia get into her "skinny" jeans is the equivalent of soft porn. All that jumping, tugging, and grunting while the smooth denim swallows up all that ass makes me hard every single time. Black-Italian women are a wonder and a prayer.

I clear my throat and throw on a T-shirt and a pair of sweatpants. "Don't take it personally, piccola ragazza. Enzo is extremely protective of her, and he trusts very few people. The fact that he's brought her here now proves you're growing on him."

She shakes her head and laughs. " It's more likely that whatever he has to tell you is desperately important, and he has no choice. I know you told them not to bother you in the mornings. You ain't slick! But I'll take it, because I love kids."

That makes me pause. " You do?"

She smiles and nods eagerly. " Of course! My mother was

a teacher, and I taught music to kids after school for years. They're so innocent and ready to learn. And when they are as small as Aria, they're full of love."

I don't know why. But hearing her say that she wants kids makes my entire body vibrate with anticipation. In my line of work, we don't have the luxury of anticipating the future. You could be here today and gone tomorrow. That comes with the territory. Our thing is all about living fast, living well, but not living long. The last part made me all but vow to never bring a child into this world that would be forced to mourn me the way I mourned my parents.

But the idea of Lucia around my child is hard to resist. Her being heavy with my seed is the ultimate sign of ownership. Not to mention, it's a serious turn-on. Having my child would finally make her completely mine. Knowing that my legacy could live even after I leave this earth is enticing. A part of me would still be in this world, and for the first time in a long time, that makes me hopeful. All at once, I want her pregnant, happy, and I'll take her barefoot if I can get it. I already want to wrap Lucia up in a cloud of indulgence and hide her away from this dark world and its disappointments. As the mother of my child, she will only bring out the caveman in me even more. I'll go crazy worrying about them being safe and protected. However, it's worth it if I can have a little bambino or bambina with her eyes in my world.

I walk over and land a tender kiss on the top of her head. "Hmm, I'm glad to hear that."

That's all I say before running to open the door. I take a quick glance back and see that Lucia's mouth has dropped open. I don't know if she's surprised that I'm glad that she likes kids or that she realizes her admission might have just invited me to plant my seed in her womb.

When I open the door, Aria jumps up and down and smiles. She extends her arms, waiting for one of my infamous bear swings.

"Mia cara!" I scream as I pick her up under her arms and whirl around in circles. Her giggles and laughter always wash away any pain and uncertainty in my life. When she came into our lives, she was a breath of fresh air. Every time she's around, she's like a drug. There are not many pure things in this life, but this little girl - she's everything good and pleasant.

Once I put her down, I hunched down to her level and looked into her eyes. "Tell Uncle Rocco what you have been doing since the last time I saw you. It's been too long, my darling."

"I know!" Aria squeals. "But you came all the way to Italy without telling me. I was still in Chicago waiting for our pancake Saturdays!"

Displaying my best face of guilt, I apologize. "I'm sorry, mia cara. Work got so busy, but we can have pancakes today if you like!"

"No! That's OK. I already had breakfast. Daddy came and got me yesterday, and we rode on the big plane."

"I look at Enzo and try to read the worry etched along his face. Something significant must be happening if he thought he needed to bring Aria from Chicago to Ravello. Leo might be causing mischief earlier than I thought.

"Well, I for one am happy you're here, and I have someone significant for you to meet."

She steps on her tippy toes to look over my shoulder and eye Lucia. I turn and watch Lucia give her a small wave and her beautiful smile.

"Is that your wife, Uncle Rocco? Daddy told me you got married. Is she a Princess?"

I laugh. "No, darling, you're a princess. She's a queen. Would you like to meet her majesty?"

"Oh yes!' she giggles.

I pick her up and walk her over to Lucia. "Lucia Fieri, meet Aria Bianchi; the love of my life.

Aria scrunches up her nose and hits my shoulder. "I can't be the love of your life, silly."

"Why not?"

"Because your queen has to be. Aren't you the king?"

While I'm at a loss for words, Lucia raises her eyebrows and laughs. I quickly changed the subject. Lucia is critical to me. She's my wife and someone I want in my life for the long haul. She's the woman I want to bear my children. But love? There's no space for love in our arrangement.

"Aria," I say. "Why don't you tell Lucia all about your American Girl Doll Collection while your daddy and I talk?"

Lucia steps right up. "Hi Aria. It's very nice to meet you. How many dolls do you have? As Lucia reaches out her hand, she shoots a glance at Mario and me to make sure everything is okay. Enzo nods, and I do too, and when Aria takes her hand and starts blabbing about her latest doll acquisition, I slip out with Enzo.

"What's going on?" I asked brusquely.

"Leo attacked your uncle's house last night. We barely got the don out, and he's badly injured. That's why I had to rush back to Italy. I can't have Aria in danger. Her nanny got killed in the blast, but she doesn't know it yet."

"Fuck, and you think this was Leo? "Does he even have the balls to blow up his father's home?"

Mario looks at me like I'm an idiot. "Rocco, if the man has balls enough to hire mercenaries and plot the demise of his own father. He would blow his house up. We even got some footage of Leo's car leaving, along with more mercenaries he has hired. Once again, they're all Armenians." Mario rubs his head and exhales. "This is getting bad. I feel like he's getting closer to us."

I shake my head. "If he knew where we were, he would attack us, not my uncle."

Enzo crosses his arms across his chest. "I'm not so sure about that. His actions feel like a diversion of sorts. I have a feeling Leo knows exactly where we are but is waiting for the right moment to strike."

I scoff. "Leo doesn't have that kind of self-control. If he knows where I am, and he knows what I'm planning, he's attacking. There's no way that hothead would wait. Is the drug swap setup? It's supposed to go down in three days. If anything, he's preparing for that."

Enzo shakes his head. "Rocco, you have a blind spot when it comes to Leo. You think the drugs and power are his prize, but it's deeper than that. This is personal for him. He hates you and his father. That kind of hate can focus a man."

I lean against the door and look at him carefully. "What the fuck are you talking about?"

"I'm talking about the fact that you still think of Leo as your idiot cousin who's been your rival since he was sixteen.

However, you need to realize that you're both grown up now and have matured into men. He may be more of a psychopath, but he's a smarter one than he was ten or twenty years ago. I'm pretty sure he knows we have Lucia, but I don't think he cares. If we're all babysitting her out here in Italy, then he can wreak as much havoc as he likes back in Chicago. He doesn't need her to get Ricci's attention if he takes out the head of the Romano family."

I stare at him. He may be right, but I'm not ready to admit that Lucia may be a diversion.

Enzo paces in front of me. "Look, I think someone else is advising him. It's all too coordinated, and he must be getting the money for all these men from someone with deep pockets. Something about this doesn't feel right, Rocco and I feel like we're missing a giant piece of the puzzle."

I straighten up and approach him. "Well, brother, isn't it you and Mario's job to put the puzzle pieces together? Lucia and I can take care of Aria today. We will keep her busy and safe. You two need to go and shake some trees and find out what my cousin is up to. It's time to put an end to this. We may need to reach out to Matteo Ricci and push up the date of our plan."

Mario looks towards the door. "Are you sure we can trust him? Can we trust her?"

"Yes, "I growl. Lucia is trustworthy. Her father wants her to be safe. Don't question her loyalty again, Enzo. She's my wife, and she doesn't have a dog in this fight. Not really. We will take care of your little girl. Just go and bring me back some news."

"Enzo nods but hesitates. I can tell he doesn't want to

leave Aria, but he knows an order when he hears one, and he leaves.

I take a moment to think about all he said. He's right about one thing; it seems that Leo is trying to divert us. I don't understand his end game or why he would attack his father directly like that. It doesn't make sense for him to show his hand this early without all the pieces in place. I have the most significant piece he's seeking, my wife.

Perhaps he is working with someone else. Maybe the Armenians aren't just mercenaries. Possibly, Leo is collaborating with them to advance his ambitions. Something is rotten in Denmark, but today I don't want to focus on that. I want to show my two girls a good time. I want Lucia to see how good it can be between us and how we can be good parents, even in this life.

I know just the way to do it. A beach day never fails.

19

LUCIA

Watching my husband run along the white sand of his private beach chasing a giggling Aria brings a calm I haven't felt since I was a child with my mother.

We often played along the rocky shore of Rockaway Beach. To me, at a young age, it may as well have been Miami's Collins or Ocean Drive. I didn't know we weren't a beach town until I discovered that some cities stay warm all year round and that the beach is always open and accessible.

My mother was happiest near water and music. Her will stated that she wished to be cremated and her ashes scattered over the Atlantic Ocean. I hated to burn her beautiful, cocoa-colored body. I wanted to do what made me feel good instead, and bury her in Woodlawn Cemetery in the Bronx, where her favorite jazz musicians, Duke Ellington, Miles Davis, and Max Roach rest in the Jazz Corner. But I kept her wishes.

This whole situation has made me think about her life in a different light. She was carrying a lot. I was angry that she left me the way she did, but I don't feel alone anymore.

"You can't catch me, Uncle Rocky!"

I smile at her cute nickname for Rocco. No one else would dare attempt it, not even me. However, I can't deny that he's as much in his element here playing tag with a four-year-old as he is hunting down the murderers, thugs, and drug dealers that come against his family. He faces daily threats from the worst of humanity, and still, he can run free on the beach with floppy Black hair, a huge smile, and dancing blue eyes like he doesn't have a care in the world. He's happy. Somehow, his happiness makes me feel a little more at ease.

Maybe, just maybe, it isn't a terrible thing that I kind of like my husband.

My kidnapper.

My lover.

We've spent the better part of the day on this private beach outside of Positano. Our morning started with lunch and swimsuit shopping in the heart of the city. We stopped by the Missoni boutique I adore. Aria and I picked out matching swimsuits and cover-ups—the colorful threads shimmer under the sun. Rocco let me pick out a funky pair of trunks for him. The bright knit lifted our moods as we headed toward his yacht, the Santa Maria, which took us to our destination.

Aria was a bit sad when Rocco came back into the room this morning after his pow-wow with Enzo. Her father was gone, and it's clear that no one compares to him in her mind. He's her safety net. I was a bit anxious because I knew only hell would tear Enzo from her. Whatever called him away must have come from the gates of hell to make him run away without saying a proper goodbye. That scares me.

But as soon as I saw the blue water, I knew there was no need to worry. I'm not in control. God is... As far and vast as this blue sea is, that's how far I am from truly knowing the exact what and why of my current situation. This experience has taught me to live in the moment and always make the most of the moments I'm gifted.

"I'll catch you, my little starfish." Rocco leans down and stretches his arms to the side like an airplane. He picks up speed and captures the little girl, hugging her tightly. "I'll always catch you, Aria, you never have to worry. You'll never be alone if your father and I are alive."

I privately wipe the tears gathering in my eyes as I watch from the spot where Aria and I were building the most fabulous sandcastle of all time. Of course, Rocco catches me, because the man sees everything. He doesn't say anything; he only nods and brushes the sand off Aria with a towel.

His words pricked my heart and caused an unexpected flood of tears. I never had a father, uncle, or any other man in my life swear to protect me. I dreamed of having a father until I was old enough to know they didn't simply appear out of desire, necessity, or want. Fathers appeared and stayed around when they cared. Mine simply never did.

But Rocco isn't interested in my childhood trauma. Not unless it serves him in some way. So, I will keep my tears to myself.

I place my hands over my eyes and look at us across the sea. It's late in the afternoon, and we probably should get back. I turn to Rocco and smile. "Are you ready to head back?"

He nods. "Yes, we are losing light, and this little munchkin is ready for dinner." He tickles her sides and she giggles. "What is it you said you wanted for dinner again, Mia Cara? Octopus legs and fish eggs?"

"No! She squeals with laughter. "I said fish sticks and French fries!"

"Oh yes!" He exclaims as he puts her down. "I must have misheard you. Let's grab all our things and head to the boat. We can't keep your little stomach waiting."

I walk up beside him to help pick up all of Aria's beach toys. "You're so good with her. It's sweet."

He pauses after throwing a bright blue shover in one of the three Goyard St. Louis Bags serving as our beach carryalls today. Living with wealth is still an adjustment for me. However, it's getting easier. I looked up the price of the colorful totes when Rocco finally gave me a phone. It was brand new and only had one number-his. However, Google works just fine, and I almost threw up in my mouth when I saw that each bag was nearly $ 2,000!

"You act surprised. Do you think I'm such a monster that I have no heart? No capacity to be "sweet," as you say? By now, I thought you understood that I am a sweet man." He moves closer to me and reaches his arm around my waist. Pulling me into him, he whispers against my ear, "I just so happen also to be a dangerous man too."

He bites the top of my ear and nips the earlobe; squeezing my ass before he runs over to help one of our maids get Aria into the yacht.

Once I get my bearings, I move towards the boat.

Do I still think he's a monster?

A month ago, that answer would have been a resounding yes. He stripped me of my environment and dreams with no warning and little explanation. He spanked my ass, disciplined me, and hurt my feelings with his cold distant demeanor. Now, I'm not so sure.

In the midst of all that, he protected me. Covered my body when we were under attack. He took me away to a safe and beautiful place where I can find refuge in the middle of a shitstorm. He pleases my body day and night, releasing any tension that's built up and spoils me rotten by introducing me to the finer things in life.

Once I'm on the boat, I look around for a few moments and find Aria inside the dining room, throwing down on her fish sticks and French fries. Rocco is sitting on a curved ivory leather sofa built into the honey wood wall of the boat. This boat is exquisite, and no detail is left unattended. He catches my eye and gestures for me to sit next to him on the couch.

I swallow. I'm falling for him, and that's the worst thing I can do, because I know he will never fall with me. He doesn't want love, he wants obedience. Trying to hold a man like Rocco to something as finite as love is like chasing a waterfall. I'll never catch him. The most I can hope for is that he will see me, dust me off, and place me back in the world with a semblance of dignity.

I need some time away from him. When he touches me, my brain short-circuits and I lose common sense. Right now, I need to call on all the common sense that my good mother instilled in me. She used to say , *Fòse moun fè sa yo pa vle fè se tankou esye plen lanmè ak wòch.* Forcing people to do what they do not want to do is like trying to fill the ocean with rocks. Now I wonder if that proverb was one of her favorites because of my father. Did she try to reach him? Did he reject her?

I walk back towards the hallway. "Umm, I was just going to take a shower and get cleaned up for dinner. I'm still dirty and wet." I close my eyes tightly, *dirty and wet. I didn't mean it like that.* Rocco chuckles.

"What if I like you dirty and wet?" My cheeks warm, and I throw a look towards Aria, who isn't paying her uncle any mind. She's too engrossed in the ketchup mountain she's creating for her French fries.

I turn back to him, and he shrugs with a smirk. He turns away from Aria and the maid, allowing his robe to open a bit. I make out the imprint of his large shaft through his knit trunks and curse under my breath. *He's not playing fair.* "Dress in something nice for me. We are having dinner on the boat tonight after Aria is put to bed. I have a surprise for you."

I nod and scurry to our room to shower. I have approximately two hours, and I need to get a power nap before I deal with the sex god I'm breaking bread with tonight. A clear head, clean body, and full belly should keep my thoughts and body at bay.

20

The sound of music leads me to my husband. Ivory keys are playing perfectly in tune as Chopin's Second Piano Concerto fills the air. The soft tinkling is timeless, and he doesn't miss a note. I assume he's the one playing since he dismissed everyone else for our dinner tonight.

This must be my surprise.

I eyed the baby grand piano when I boarded the yacht earlier today. I wondered if he was the one who played it. Regardless of the answer, I never thought he would play for me. Not after the reaction I got when I asked him to play after our first dinner in Ravello.

When I turn the corner, I see him. He's seated at the bench in a black suit with his tanned fingers deftly flying across the keys. He's good. Rocco didn't lie when he said he was once one of the best in the world. I can believe it. This is a challenging piece to play, and he's executing it without a misstep.

I sit down on a nearby chair and am mesmerized by his skill. He glances up at me once with warmth and approval in his eyes, and I'm glad I obeyed his dress code.

I'm wearing a sleek Black Versace silk dress with a deep V in the front that barely covers my breasts, with a backless view from behind. The high split up my right thigh is nearly indecent, but my gams look damn good in it. The dress feels special, luxurious, and ideally suited for this private concert.

Rocco's face is awash with peace, and I realize this is his quiet space, and he rarely lets anyone in. But I'm inside his bubble, and right now I'll do anything to stay.

When the Concerto ends, I'm sad. I was adrift with him inside the music, the way only a true musician understands. He stands and holds his hand out for me to join him at the piano bench.

"You're an amazing musician, Rocco," I say as I walk towards him. He gestures for me to have a seat at the bench before leaning down and landing a kiss on my temple.

"Thank you," he mutters as he joins me on the bench. "I'm no Lucia Asare Parisi, but" he shrugs and feigns deference, "I'll do. You look beautiful tonight, Lucia. Thank you for wearing the dress I selected."

I warm under his praise, and I hate that it feels so good. I will not overthink anything tonight. Right now, I want to enjoy my husband and the fact that he thinks I'm beautiful in the dress that he picked out just for me.

"Thank you." I inhale a deep breath as I try not to squirm under his intense gaze. He's looking at me like I'm a prize he's finally won, and I don't quite know what to do with all the attention. "So, what now? Was this my surprise?"

He nods, "Yes, it was. I rarely let anyone hear me play anymore."

I laugh. "Yes, I figured that. But it seems like behind a piano is your happy place."

He takes my hand and gently kisses every knuckle before speaking.

"Forgive me for how I handled things, Lucia."

His voice is low, quiet—but it pulls my eyes to him like a tether. He stands there, shoulders broad and tense, as if the words cost him more than he wants to admit.

"I wish I could tell you I was just scared, or trying to protect you. But that would be a lie. I was an asshole. I didn't trust you. I took you because my uncle ordered it. I married you because it made sense—for the sake of the family. For taking Leo down. You were leverage. Nothing more."

He pauses, like the next part might choke him.

"But the second you walked into my basement, everything shifted. You mattered more than the mission, and I hated that. I hated how fast I wanted you, for more than strategy. So I tried to shut it down. Push you away. It didn't work."

I blink at him, stunned and silent for a beat.

"Why?" I finally asked, my voice barely above a whisper. "Why would you hate that?"

He exhales slowly, eyes shadowed.

"Because when I was sixteen, I learned that wanting something that bad means watching it burn."

There's something haunted in his tone. I inch closer.

"What happened?"

"My father was weak," he says. "He wasn't a made man. Claimed he didn't want a life in the Mafia, but he married my mother, Maria Romano. Thomasso's youngest sister. That made escape impossible. My uncle never thought he was good enough for her, and my father resented him for it. It made him desperate for power, for approval. For any sign that he was more than what he was."

Rocco's jaw tightens.

"He slept around. Took comfort in whores that made him feel like a man. One of those women was the daughter of a Ricci soldier. A fucking spy. She gave Ricci the location of our safe house. Matteo was young then, looking to make a name for himself. He had my parents killed. A message to my uncle."

My hand covers my mouth. "Jesus, Rocco..."

"I was sixteen. I watched the fire from the sidewalk. My hands still smelled like piano keys. I never played again after that night. If my sainted mother, a gifted pianist herself, could no longer hear me-no, no one could."

His voice dips, full of pain. "Thomasso took me in. Raised me with Leo and Luna. By seventeen, I was a made man. By twenty-one, a killer."

"But you're not just muscle," I say, needing to understand more of him. "I've heard you talk. You're... calculated. Educated."

A small, bitter smile tugs at his lips.

"My uncle had a plan. He kept me off the streets. Made me finish school. Four years at Princeton. Three more at Harvard

Law. While Leo beat men to prove he was tough, I was studying tax codes and zoning permits. I've beaten murder cases, negotiated labor contracts, and laundered millions in dirty money so clean it sparkles. I'm not just Consigliere—I'm the brain that keeps the Romano empire untouchable."

"And yet," I whisper, "you cook for me. You hold me when I'm scared. You play piano when no one's watching."

He flinches.

"I don't play anymore."

"But you do," I say gently. "I heard you."

His jaw clenches.

"It's a weakness. And I don't have room for weakness. Not when Leo's building his army. Not when you've become the one thing I can't afford to lose."

I cross the room and stand in front of him, unsure what I'm doing. Uncertain what he'll do.

"You're not weak, Rocco. You're just... human."

He looks at me like no one ever dared say that to his face before.

"I buried my parents. I burned my past. I built a life on blood and fire. But you?"

He reaches out, his fingers barely brushing my cheek.

"You terrify me, Lucia. Because for the first time, I don't want to win if it means losing something precious to me."

My breath catches in my throat as his strokes up and down my arm leave goosebumps in their wake.

"Now, piccolo ragazza, will you play for me?"

After hearing the closest thing I think Rocco will ever say to me —'I love you' — my mouth is dry and my ears are buzzing. *He's wanted me from the beginning? Does he like me?* When I finally clear my head, I answer.

"Of course, what would you like to hear? Maybe some Mozart or Beethoven?

He shakes his head, "No, I'd like to hear something you've composed. I know you have songs because my men found your notebooks amongst your things when they cleaned out your apartment. I want to say I'm sorry for snooping, but I'm not. It was the only way I could learn anything about you. I was trying to make your stay with me as painless as possible.

Rocco is being so soft and tender with me right now, so I decide to let the blatant violation of my privacy go. Now I understand why all my favorite foods and drinks were always readily available. He knew what I liked, and he made sure I had it. He tried to make a terrible situation bearable. Something about that makes me feel good inside.

"OK, I'll play something original for you, but I'll warn you. All my stuff is jazzy, not classical. Are you ready for some good old-fashioned Black music? Think Thelonious Monk meets Hazel Scott.

He smirks. "I'm more than ready for anything that you give me."

I swallow and focus my attention on the keys in front of me so that I don't do something crazy like grab and kiss him breathless. We're still technically on shaky ground, but it's becoming more solid every day. I launch into Mama, the last piece I wrote before I was kidnapped.

The melody begins bright but quickly turns somber and heavy. I thump the keys like I'm trying to reincarnate the only woman who ever loved me unconditionally. The woman who brought me life, but is no longer present in mine. It's not long before the tears come, and Rocco wipes them away, one by one. As I continue to play and cry, not one tear hits the keys.

I weep for a mother and a father I've never known. I wail on these keys for having no place in this world that I can call my own. I belong to a husband I barely know, but who's quickly becoming my lifeline. This is dangerous.

As I continue to play his hands began to sweep over my body and I feel his fingertips creep up the slit of my dress and between my thighs. I tense, but I never stop playing. On and on, the notes of the piano fill the room as his fingertips fill my body. His hand rubs across my clit and I moan into the sounds that come from the piano.

"Don't come," he whispers. "Keep playing."

Fuck, I need to come...

I bite my bottom lip as he adds another finger inside me, and I play like my life depends on it. I play as if I won't get to come if this song doesn't, please him. His fingers move in and out of me in rhythm with my heart song. When I hear the rip of my dress, I gasp, but I don't stop playing. Now., I'm playing in only a black bra and silk pooled around my thong-clad ass. It's only when he stands up behind me and places his hands over mine that I stop playing and catch my panting breath.

His low voice whispers in my ear. "Now I'm going to fuck you on top of this piano because it's all I've wanted to do since I've brought you aboard this yacht. Then I'm going to carry you into our bedroom and hold you while you tell me everything that's made you cry. I want to know why you were crying on the beach today, and I want to take away everything that hurts you.

My voice cracks with pain. "You can't, because she's gone.

He places a finger over my lips. "Shhh. Yes, she is, but I'm here and you'll never be alone again."

He picks me up and lays me across the piano before undressing and climbing up to join me. He lays his body over mine, wrapping his arms around my back. He presses our lips together before gliding into me with one easy stroke, and I cry out from the pleasure.

"That's it, beautiful, take all of me. Ti senti incredibile..." he groans into my ear. I don't understand much Italian but I know he just praised my pussy.

His kisses continue all over my body. His lips brush my eyes, my nose, my neck, and my breasts before returning to my mouth in a sloppy and wet massage. I know the expensive black lacquer of this piano is being covered in a torrential rain as I scream and cream all around his cock. My hands fling out and land on the keys below us, banging out a chaotic melody, I'll never forget.

I come like a burst of light in the night sky.

"That's it, Lucia," he moans. "Let me fuck your Blues away. Come on my dick and then come to me with your heart's sorrow."

I come again, and this time he joins me in a roar. Then we lie there together, a breathless puddle of bliss.

When we catch our breath, he climbs down from the piano and scoops me up in his arms. He carries us to our room and puts me down next to the bed. Pulling the covers back, he gestures for me to climb in and follows behind.

"Now, tell me why you were crying at the beach."

I pause for a moment. I'm not sure if I should be this vulnerable with him. Can I trust him with my disappointments?

He senses my unease and kisses my ear. "Piccola ragazza, you can trust me. I only want to make you happy. Tell me what or who's making you cry; I'll kill them.

I sigh, determined not to cry again. I'm all cried out. Plus, he's making me laugh.

"I just heard you talking to Aria earlier about how she'll always have you and Mario, and I thought about how I don't have anyone like that in my life anymore. I never had a father, or a man to tell me those things you were telling her, and it just made me wonder why my father never wanted me. I mean, I guess he had his reasons, and my mother had hers. But if he knew I was born, then he must know that she died. He didn't even reach out. He didn't even leave me a letter or a note to let me know that the money would continue to come. It's like I don't even exist to him. I don't know; it just brought up all these emotions that I wasn't ready for.

"Fucking Ricci bastard." Rocco clenches his teeth and whispers under his breath. "Lucia, trust me. I've met the man, and it's his loss, not yours.

That makes me smile, and he looks pleased with himself.

"If I didn't think it would start a war, I'd kill the man myself for hurting you."

I pull away and look at him."

"What! I don't want you to kill my father, Rocco."

He chuckles. "I know. Just know I'll do anything for you, including kill anyone who hurts you. You're mine, Lucia, and I take care of what's mine. I'll never break your heart, at least not on purpose."

I look into his eyes, trying to find the truth in his words. "But what if you're the one who hurts me?

He looks wounded by my insinuation. He reaches his hand out and rubs my cheek. How could I hurt you, mia cara?"

"By lying to me," I answer quickly. "By telling me all these things and not meaning a word."

His hand squeezes my hip underneath the covers. "Lucia, I've told you. I don't lie, and I would never lie to you."

I look into his ice blue eyes. "So, this whole marriage, you've only told me the truth?"

He pauses, and at first, I think he's going to confess something. Then his face relaxes into the stone surety I've come to expect. "No, Lucia, I've never lied to you. I've only told you the truth because that was the best way to keep you safe. You needed to know the score. I don't know what's happening between Lucia and me, and I'm not even entirely sure of what I'm feeling. I don't have flowery words or confessions of love, but I do know you're becoming the most important thing to me and that I will never let the world harm you. I'd rather cut out my own heart than break yours."

For the first time, I pull him into me and kiss him with all my might. I take charge, and he lets me as my tongue delivers long strokes to his mouth. I want him, and I push him flat on his back.

"Well, husband, for that declaration, I think you deserve a ride."

He places his hands behind his head and gives me a boyish grin. "Oh, I deserve much more than that and I plan to get everything owed to me out of that beautiful ass of yours."

I chuckle as I slide down his body wanting to taste him first, but a loud siren goes off and I jump off the bed. Rocco whispers, "Get down."

I obey immediately and lie flat on my stomach next to the bed. He pulls on a pair of boxers and reaches behind the headboard. He pulls a Glock out and stalks towards the door.

God, there's probably guns and ammunition all over this boat. But right now, I'm grateful for the NRA and all its intense lobbying.

"You stay here," Rocco hisses. "Don't move until I come and get you."

I nod as tears come down my face. He runs over and bends down to kiss my head. "No tears, Lucia, I will protect you." Then he's gone.

This is the second time we've been attacked amid making love, and I can't help but think it's some omen. I stayed down for about twenty minutes, and I heard nothing, no noise. Ten minutes more and the silence is becoming too much. What if he's hurt? Why hasn't anyone busted into this room to get me if he's down? *What if it's Leo?!*

I can't just stay here. He told me to, but it doesn't feel safe anymore. There have to be more guns in this room some-where. Slowly, I stand up and look around. Sure enough, I find a safe. I think about what the combination could be and remember Aria telling me her birthday was March 4th. She was born in 2018. I turn the numbers on the dial until I hear a satisfactory click, and then it opens.

Sure enough, there's another Glock and a smaller pistol. Seeing that I've never shot anything in my life; I think the gun is my best bet. I throw on a robe and tiptoe out of the room.

The closer I get to the great room where we made love on top of the piano, the more I hear voices.

One voice is that of my husband, and the other I don't recognize. Their voices are growing louder, and the stranger is becoming increasingly agitated. I hold the gun tight, thinking I might have to shoot.

What if I have to save my husband's life?

But then I hear the unknown voice say something that knocks the breath out of my chest.

"Bring me my daughter Fieri. You can't keep me from Lucia any longer. I told you I was coming for her. She belongs to me, I'm her blood."

Then my world shatters, again.

21

ROCCO

I feel her presence the moment Lucia is nearby.

That's the way it's become between us over the past few weeks.

In Jane Eyre, there's a moment where Mr. Rochester tells Jane that he feels the presence of an invisible string connecting the two beneath his left rib. He claims with fervor that if that tether ever snapped, he'd bleed inwardly while she would forget he ever existed. Rochester was old, hardened by the world, and prone to outbursts of anger, while Jane was young, innocent, and talented. The world before her, his criminal past behind him; if he didn't protect the frailty of that string with his life, then he would lose her forever.

When I first read it, I thought it was sentimental dribble. I saw it as a passage of words to get through to reach the end of the book. At this moment, I have a different view of that passage. Charlotte Brontë herself must have felt that snap;

she was an emotional savant. I feel the snap of the string that kept Lucia in my universe the moment I hear her soft steps turn the corner. She's holding my mother's pistol, and it seems fitting. I'd want her to have it.

My silly, brave, and disobedient girl.

The betrayal in her eyes lets me know that she heard what the bastard just said and she's more than pissed. She's hurt. I lied to her, now she'll be more determined than ever to escape. Too bad, I'll never let her go. I need her too much. My need has nothing to do with the Roman Ascension but everything to do with the warmth of her sun. I won't live in the cold without it.

"Father?" Her eyes stay focused on me, and I realize she's asking me if what she heard is true. Even now, she's praying I'm not as monstrous as I appear to be. But I am.

I'm dismissed before I can even respond. Her attention turns to Matteo as she closes in on the truth.,

"You're Matteo Ricci?" Her voice is strong and sure. Her chin held high, she faces the man who created and abandoned her.

Matteo eyes her carefully. He assesses her with a detached interest. I wonder if she feels it. I pray to God her anger at me does not distort her discernment. That's a skill I've admired her for since we met. She read me like a book within moments of meeting me.

"I am. Come closer, child. I want to have a good look at you."

"Stay right where you are." I bark. "Don't move."

Matteo scowls. "Is this how you've been treating my daughter? Like some dog you can call. She's a Ricci, and she should be treated like a queen, something you promised you would do."

His feigned care is starting to get under my skin. He's up to something, and I'm not letting Lucia anywhere near him until I know exactly what it is. Matteo is a dangerous and unpredictable man. It was one thing for him to want her back because she's his. That's the mafia way. I expect that from a man like him. It's something else entirely if he attaches value to her. Assets can be traded or sacrificed like pawns on a chessboard.

"I treat her like my wife. I promised you that I wouldn't kill her and that she would want for nothing. The former is not a promise I can guarantee will apply to you unless you tell me what the fuck you are doing on my boat. We had a deal and you're breaking it."

Lucia jumps between us and glares in both our directions before fixing her eyes on me. "What deal are you talking about, Rocco? You told me you hadn't heard from my father. That he hadn't reached out. Are you now telling me that he knew I was with you the entire time?"

The hurt in her eyes nearly brings me to my knees. I don't have an answer for her. I wasn't prepared for this confrontation. She could never understand why I kept her father from her because she doesn't understand this life. She still thinks their father-daughter bond means something, but I know it can easily mean her death.

She snaps her head around and levels her stare on Matteo before I can answer. "And you. Did you sell me to him or something? Is this deal about money? I'm not a commodity to be sold. Somebody needs to tell me what the fuck is going on!"

"Language," I growl.

She laughs. "Fuck you Rocco and your dominating bullshit. You're a liar, and you know how I feel about those."

"Enough." Matteo barks. "You will learn respect once you're in my house. I did not trade you for money. I didn't even know Fieri had you until my men surveilled him kidnapping you."

"You were following me?" Lucia asks with equal amounts of disgust and hope. It breaks my heart. She wants to know that her father cared enough about her to have her followed. I pray he can't smell the desperation, because men like him only exploit that kind of optimism. As expected, he continues with his line of bullshit.

"Of course, daughter. I always kept tabs on you. There were always men watching for your safety."

He never kept a crew of men surveilling her. He kept surveillance on me, and that's how he found her. But this isn't the time to point this out to Lucia, so I keep my mouth shut. She won't believe me anyway. Right now, she's too angry to listen.

She no longer trusts me.

Once her father senses her hanging onto his every word, he continues to weave a lie around her mind. Circling us both, he continues.

"When I saw that Rocco Fieri, the consigliere of Thomasso Romano, kidnapped you from your home, I figured they were trying to get something out of me. You see, dolce figlia, we're old enemies. Our world may still be a mystery to you, but you must understand that our two families are always a misunderstanding away from war. So naturally I thought this was the way his uncle decided to shake things up, after what Rocco? Twenty years of peace?"

I want to knock that sly grin off his face. The only reason I don't is Lucia. If it weren't for her, not even his two soldiers could stop me. She wouldn't understand. He's baiting me right now, but he won't win.

"When I attempted to rescue you from that god awful safehouse he had you in, little did I know he'd already married you."

Lucia's face turns bright red with anger as she rushes over and pushes me. "That was my father trying to rescue me? You let me believe that that was Leo coming to take me away. How could you? "she hisses.

The anger in her voice is only eclipsed by the pain she feels. I allow her to keep hitting my shoulders. I want her to release her rage, but when her hands head toward my face, I grab her wrist. "NO!"

"I never told you that Leo was the one who bombed the safehouse. I told you I suspected it was him. It wasn't until we were back in Italy that I found out it wasn't. Enzo got the Intel and realized it must have been someone else. Then your father called and made demands."

"I demanded to see my daughter."

I turn to Matteo with a lethal glare. "You demanded that I return what's yours. But she was never yours... was she? You never gave enough of a damn to call her in twenty-four years. All I did was take a neglected rosebud and nurture it. I watched her bloom more in a month under my care than she ever did with an absentee dad.

Lucia scoffs. Are you trying to act like you're noble? You lied to me and tricked me into marrying you!"

I crowd her delicious body so she can feel my presence. "I never tricked you. You were in danger. I got to you before Leo did. Your father wasn't looking for you until he knew I had you. He would have let Leo do the same thing because he was surveilling us, not you. The difference being if Leo captured you, I'm not sure you would have survived."

Mateo begins a slow clap that turns into a hard chuckle. "Excellent, Rocco. That's quite the story you've spun. However, I've been investigating the claims you've made about your cousin, and they don't add up. Sure, Leo's a wayward son. He's a little upset at his father. Who wouldn't be when he gives the second in command to his orphaned nephew instead of his only son? Even that bitch Luna would have been a better choice than you."

He spits Luna's name out like she's a bad taste in his mouth, and I smirk. He's still pissed that she grazed his left and right knee from five hundred feet away a year ago after he smacked her ass in a restaurant. She didn't tell Uncle Thomasso because she wasn't supposed to be in that Bratva-owned bar in the first place, and she wanted her justice.

She took those shots at Matteo and spared his knees to prove that she could. And to avoid a war, of course. She's a psycho just like her brother, but a lovable one with honor. Now I wish Luna had just taken this bastard out. He's up to something, and I will find out what it is before he can hurt my Lucia any more than he already has.

He continues his monologue while pouring himself a drink at my bar. He's touching my shit like he owns it and it's making my trigger finger itch. "You know what I think, Rocco. I think you want the Romano throne for yourself. How do we know you're not the one trying to remove your uncle from the picture? I want peace in our streets, so you leveraged my daughter to get my ear. Once I realized what your game was, I tracked you down here."

I walk over and snatch my bourbon from his hands midpour. He growls but knows not to push too far. My men have arrived, and they are armed to the teeth.

"You're full of shit Matteo. You know damn well what Leo's capable of and you know I have no intentions of overthrowing my uncle. If that were the case, why didn't you contact him before you came here?

"How do you know I didn't?" He bites back.

I smile. "Because I called him the moment I stepped out of my bedroom. The funny thing is, he couldn't answer, but our capo, Enzo, did. It seems no one has seen him since his house was blown up two days ago."

Lucia gasps. "The Don's house was bombed?" Her eyes frantically search mine. "Who did that?"

"Yes, Rocco, who did that?" Her father echoes.

"I assumed it was Leo, but now I'm not so sure."

He grunts. "Leo is a very convenient excuse for you, isn't he? What else have you blamed on him throughout the years? I've seen how close you are to that little bastard Aria, is she yours? Maybe you're the one that knocked that slut Caterina up."

I lunge at his throat, and our men prepare for battle. "You

keep her name out of your filthy mouth, old man, or I swear to God I'll kill you with my bare hands." I snarl.

"No Rocco!" Lucia yells as she points the pistol at me.

Would she do it? Would she shoot me to save her bastard of a father?

"Both of you just STOP!" She screams, and I drop my fingers from Matteo's neck. He coughs and catches his breath, cursing me the entire time. I turn back to Lucia, and the gun is shaking in her hand. This could go south quickly if I don't get control of the situation.

"Give me the gun, la mia Lucia palla di fuoco. Just give me the gun, and this can all be cleared up."

She shakes her head. "You don't get to call me that anymore, LIAR!" She drops the gun to the floor and begins to sob. "This is all too much. I don't know how I became the center of a blood feud, but I'm done! I'm done with all the lies, violence, and schemes. I just want to go back to my home in Chicago, grieve my mother, and play my fucking piano in peace."

Matteo shakes his head. "Impossible. The only place that's safe for you right now is by your father's side. I tried to come to you as soon as I thought you were in danger. Rocco kept me from you, but now I'm here. Come home with me. I know I haven't been there for most of your life, but I did try to provide for you. The least I can do is provide you with a safe space to think. When all of this is over, and we find out who the true villain is, you can decide if you even want to be married to this liar anymore."

When Lucia looks at me, I know that I'm losing. This is what she always wanted: to get to know her father. It doesn't help that she also wants to get away from me. But can I let her leave this boat? I could stop her if I wanted to, but I know that would only add fuel to Matteo's fire. He knows that I care about her, but he might think it's limited to the fact that she's mine. No real Romano man will let you take what's his. He doesn't know I love her. Shit, I didn't even know that 24 hours ago. If I go batshit crazy right now; he will know. Then he'll use that to extort me for his end game. Whatever that may be.

"Do you want to go with your father?" I slowly grind out the words. Everything in my body warns me not to let her leave this boat. But what can I do?

Lucia takes a deep breath and wraps her arms around herself. "I need to be away from you. You lied to me, Rocco, something you promised me that you'd never do. I feel like I don't even know who you are anymore."

I get to her in two steps and press my body against hers. "I am your husband, and that remains true till the day you die. You can go with your father to get over your hard feelings and count all the ways that you think you hate me, but deep down, you know who you belong to." I press a hard and quick kiss to her mouth. "If you need me, you call me." I pick up my mother's gun and press it into her hands.

Matteo scoffs. "Why would she need you when she finally has me? Her flesh and blood. I can have your marriage annulled by the end of the week if she likes."

I laugh." Good luck with that older man. I don't know under what grounds you would accomplish that since I have thoroughly fucked your daughter in every way imaginable and she could very well be carrying my seed now. So, if you think you're going to keep her from me, you're wrong. I'm only letting her go because she needs this. But don't think for a second you're taking her away from me.

Lucia throws up her hands and sighs. "Don't I have a say in who I belong to? No one owns me!"

I lick the side of her face and squeeze the back of her neck. The whimper she releases makes my cock throb.

"That's where you're wrong, piccolo ragazza. I thought you knew; you are bone of my bone and flesh of my flesh. We are one."

Matteo walks behind Lucia. "If you don't let her leave and make the decision on her own, there will be consequences, Parisi. The stunt you pulled is already gone too far. My mercy won't extend much further. The only reason you aren't dead is for your uncle's sake.

I land one last soft kiss on Lucia's. Then I confront Matteo. His men crowd around him, but I don't give a fuck. "Ricci, I don't know what you're up to, but if one hair on her head is damaged, I'll personally break every bone in your body. You will die so slowly and painfully that only your dogs will hear your last screams of mercy."

He only stares for a moment before turning on his heel to walk away. Then he pauses for a moment to call for my wife over his shoulder. She glances at me with an expression I can't name before following behind him.

She'll be back...

22

My mother warned that my temper would lead me to make reckless decisions.

She hated wearing any emotion on her sleeve, including anger.

Chrisette Asare took the phrase "never let them see you sweat" to an entirely different level.

Once, she was suspended from the part-time taxi driving service she worked for because she kicked a man who was verbally assaulting her from the back of her cab. He filed a complaint, and she shared a video of the situation. I asked her why she wasn't angry about the injustice of it all. I wanted to know why she wasn't raging or plotting her revenge. She looked at me and said, 'When any emotion takes you over, your brain takes a back seat.'

In other words, you're just hot and dumb.

I wish I remembered her words before deciding to leave

the relative safety of Rocco's yacht in order to join my father, a stranger.

The anger I had towards Rocco for lying to me was all that I could think about at the time. I was determined to get away from him. I didn't want to see his face.

Although if I'm honest, that's not why I left. I wanted him to hurt as much as I did. I left because I knew that would piss him off more than anything else. He's a control freak and leaving was the ultimate fuck you.

I was so angry that I didn't stop to think about how I was handing myself over on a silver platter to a man I didn't know. My father is the head of one of the largest criminal organizations in the world, and I waltzed off that boat with him like he was Mr. Rogers.

Stupid...Stupid...Stupid...

We walked off Rocco's yacht three days ago, and I haven't heard anything from my husband since. I hate to admit it, but I miss him, even if he is a lying sack of shit. He's become familiar and comforting in a sick sort of way. In the last few weeks, he has been my entire world, and there was some peace in knowing that. But all it takes is the memory of walking up on him and my father to make me see red.

I get so upset that I feel my heart boil from anger. How could a man whom I allowed to tear down my walls of distrust look me in the eye day after day and lie? I gave him access to my body and opened my heart up to him. I shared my dreams and desires, things I've never shared with anyone. I talked to him about how much I missed having a father in my life. He held me while I cried, knowing the whole time that my father was looking for me. If I ever needed proof that the Mafia will always come before me and our marriage, that was it.

When we left the boat and entered my father's armored SUV, it didn't hit me that I was walking into another minefield until I was sitting next to him on the back seat. His whole demeanor shifted.

On the boat, he engaged me. He implored me to come, but before we got in the car, one of his men roughly took Rocco's mother's gun from me. In the car, he moved to his side of the seat and left me alone. His attention was on his phone. What oozed off him was a desire to be left alone and not questioned. But that was too fucking bad for him. I had twenty-four years' worth of questions to ask, but I started small.

"Where are we going? "I asked.

"The hotel I'm staying at," he mumbled, never looking up from his phone. "You will stay in the room I have for you there until we fly back to New York tomorrow."

My head snapped to the side. "What about Leo and all the danger there? Rocco brought me to Italy to keep me safe."

The look on my father's face could have smelled iron. "No, that piece of shit brought you to Italy to keep you away from me. To take what's mine." The last line was growled more than spoken.

I opened my mouth to say something in response. I wanted to tell him that I belonged to no one, least of all him. A man who abandoned me while I was still in utero. But the look he gave me advised me that I should probably remain quiet.

As he promised, the next day we left for New York, and he

never said another word to me. When we arrived at his Upper East Side home, I was shown to my room and dropped off like a piece of luggage. We eat our meals promptly at 8, 12, and 8. His men are always present, their faces implacable and their guns loaded.

For the past two days, we've eaten at a long mahogany dining room table in silence.

The first night, I cried through the first course of dinner, thinking about what took place on Rocco's Mahogany dining room table, our first night dining together. My father never asked me if I was ok. He continued to carve his bloody red ribeye up like a carcass. That only made me cry harder. Rocco was an asshole, but he never could stand my tears.

Last night, I heard his silverware crash down onto his plate. "If you can't make it through dinner without sniveling over a man that lied and betrayed you, then you can just go to bed." His voice was so low that the hiss made my skin crawl.

Breakfast this morning was no better. After eating in uncomfortable silence for twenty minutes, he spoke. "Tonight, you will tell me everything you learned about Romano's operations while you were in that animal's house. They will pay for taking you from me." Then he left.

All the man cares about is that something was taken from him. I'm a piece of property to him. He has no desire to get to know me. I was a fool to go with him.

I hadn't felt like a prisoner with Rocco once we arrived in Ravello. I wasn't where I wanted to be, but I didn't feel captured. With my father, that's exactly how I feel. My bedroom door locks from the outside and my windows are screwed shut. I have the run of the house, but there's always a shadow following me.

Tonight, he's called me down to join him for dinner, and if he wants to talk about Rocco, he will be disappointed. I know nothing of Rocco's plans or operations.

It's funny, when I was with him, I hated the lack of information. Now I am grateful for it. It was yet another way he protected me. If I had information, I wouldn't share it. Rocco may be on the top of my shit list right now for lying and tricking me into an unnecessary marriage; but I won't see him hurt. Anything I tell my father about my husband will end in bloodshed.

I think it's best if I take my dinner in my room tonight. I'm going to run a bath and read the newest book in Serena Akeroyd's Filthy Series. The irony of loving mafia romances is not lost upon me. But then again, what I have with Rocco can hardly be called a romance. It's more like an accommodating nightmare.

I'm in no mood to face a confrontation tonight. I want to get to know my father, but I won't subject myself to duress. He's not making it easy for me to love him. He's hard, demanding, and completely self-absorbed. I wonder what my mother ever saw in him. Then again, what they had was a fling and a mistake as far as he's concerned. Since we've gotten back to Chicago, he's done everything in his power to make me feel like a guest in his house, not a daughter.

When the housekeeper comes to the door to remind me of dinner, I tell her I'm skipping it. Her face betrays the terror she feels at having to deliver that news. She's scared of my father, but I'm not. If he wants to have dinner with me so bad, then he can just come and get me himself. I don't think he's even been on this floor since I came here. He avoids me like the plague.

I walk into my bathroom to start my bathwater when I hear a knock on my door. It must be the housekeeper again. No matter how much she begs, I'm not going down there to meet him for dinner. I sigh and run over to the door, but I'm shocked when I open it and see my father standing there.

He's a striking man. He's sixty years old, but he doesn't look a day over forty-five. His olive skin is wrinkle-free, and his jet-black hair only grays at the temples. I share his straight nose and full lips. We both carry bright brown eyes and a widow's peak. Matteo Ricci is my father; there's no denying that.

He doesn't look happy to be standing at my door. He seems downright pissed. But I don't give a fuck. He's been back in my life for all of three days; I don't have to jump every time he calls.

'Why are you not downstairs for dinner? I specifically told you we had something to discuss."

I cross my arms over my chest and look him straight in the eye. "I know what you want to discuss, and I'm not interested in that conversation. Instead of fighting, I decided it would be best to dine alone tonight."

My father narrows his eyes, and he speaks in a voice so low I barely hear him. "Get dressed and be downstairs in five minutes. We have company. He came to meet you, so it's rude to stay in your room."

I scoff. "Who is here to see me? Rocco?"

His eyes darken. "I would never let that dog in my house,

and you would do best to forget him. His name shouldn't even be on your lips. You're a Ricci, not a Romano whore."

The heat in my gut rises my neck and I rage. "Fuck you! Rocco is my husband, and he may be a lying bastard, but he's done more for me than you have at this point in my life! I'm not eating dinner with you or anyone else, so you may as well leave."

The slap stuns me. It's quick, hard, and draws blood. I'm not entirely sure he didn't knock a tooth loose. I've never been hit a day in my life, and the violence of his response shakes me to my core. I should never have come here.

I hold my jaw and eye him with tears trickling down my cheek.

I can't believe this bastard made me cry.

He adjusts his cufflinks and speaks without sparing another glance. "You will be downstairs in five minutes in the dress I left for you in the closet. If you disobey me again, I will lock you in one of my cells downstairs until you come to your senses. Curse me again, and I will end you."

He turns and leaves without another word, while I'm left stunned, rubbing my cheek. What am I going to do? I thought Rocco was a monster, but he'd never assault me. Sure, he'd spank my ass if I got a little out of line but we both knew that I liked it. He never harmed me, and yet I left the safety of his care to live with this monster. How the hell am I going to escape my father?

I'm going to have to leave here, but now, I need to play the part of the contrite daughter. Am I still in danger from Leo? Is my father negotiating with Rocco to send me back for a higher price? This is a shit show and I'm the reluctant star.

I slip on the modest red wrap dress that my father left for me in the closet. When I got to New York, casual clothes were ordered for me to lounge around the house in. I asked my father about the possibility of going to my house to retrieve some of my things, but he only grunted and said, "It's impossible." Since then, everything I've worn has been picked out by him. He made me burn the things I was wearing on the boat because Rocco had given them to me. At the time, I was mad, but I enjoyed the little bonfire. Now, I'd do anything just to be comforted by his scent.

As I walk down the steps, I hear two voices in the dining room. I'm not in the mood to entertain strangers, and I wish my father had warned me that we were having guests. Then again, I know better. I've learned over the past two weeks that these mafia men do whatever they want, whenever they want, without considering the interests of any other party, especially if you're a woman.

Head held high and shoulders back, I make my way down the stairs and enter the dining room. My father doesn't stop talking or acknowledge me when I enter, but the man with him does. He's a big man, tall and stocky. He's not out of shape, but he's not in shape either. Something about him appears undisciplined. His dirty blonde hair is long but disheveled. His green eyes spark with malice. His clothes are ill-fitting, and he looks like he doesn't belong in this perfect prison my father calls his home.

He's looking at me like I'm his next meal, and my stomach starts to churn.

Who is this man, and what does he want?

When I decide to turn around and go back upstairs, my father acknowledges my presence.

"Lucia, come to me, child. There's someone I'd like you to meet."

I take in a deep breath and plaster on my best smile. I don't want to be introduced to the slimy man tossing back a drink next to my father, but I know there's no telling Matteo Ricci no. I've tried to impose my will in different ways over the past three days, but the man doesn't budge once he gives a directive. Now that I know he can also be violent, I must move carefully.

"Of course," I say as I walk towards them. When I'm close, my father reaches out and grabs my wrist urgently. He's holding onto me like I might run at any moment. What is he about to tell me that's got him so cautious? Who is this man?

"She's beautiful, Matteo. Like an orchid freshly bloomed in Spring."

His eyes roam over my body as he speaks. Instinctively, I cross my arms over my chest for protection.

My father laughs. "Yes, it's her mother's Ghanaian heritage that makes her such a beauty. If that asshole Fieri hadn't kidnapped her and forced a marriage, her bride price would have been very high."

I open my mouth to tell him that I'm not a commodity to be bought or sold, but he squeezes my wrist to the point of pain, and I relent.

There's something recognizable around his eyes. I can't put my finger on it, but he looks familiar. He also reeks of tobacco. As he approaches, I almost choke on the stench.

When he reaches out and strokes my cheek, I recoil. My father twists my wrist, and I grimace. The stranger chuckles darkly.

"Let her go, Matteo, she won't run. Where would she go?"

Run, why would I run?

He licks his lips and circles me like prey. "Yes, she will do. My cousin thinks he's so smart, but I've outsmarted him. By the end of the night, I will own his kingdom and his wife. Maybe I'll make him watch me fuck you until you scream before I kill him."

I smack his hand away from my face and begin to tremble as I register what he said.

His cousin?

"Who are you?" I whisper, already knowing the answer.

"Oh, Bella, I'm your future." he holds his hand out for me to shake, but I ignore it. My snub doesn't stop his sneer or his following announcement.

"I'm Leo Romano, the key to your future."

I step back and shake my head no. "You will never touch me, and I'd never marry a monster like you, no matter what happens between Rocco and me."

My father scoffs. "Oh dear, don't worry, Leo will not fuck or marry you unless he can afford you. I plan to place a very high price on your pretty head, even if your hymen isn't intact. Don't you know an alliance with your papa is worth more than gold? Romano barely has enough for the drugs he's buying off me."

Leo's snarl is feral. "Watch how you speak about me, old man. We had a deal."

My father quickly pulls a gun and points it towards Leo. "Yes, and your end of the bargain is done. I have enough information to overthrow your father, and I have my daughter back. She's the biggest bargaining piece for complete power that I have. Why should I keep you alive?"

Leo doesn't flinch at the weapon. Meanwhile I'm shaking like goddamn leaf in the wind. Instead, he smiles.

"Because if I'm not returned to Sicily in exactly one week intact, recordings of all your schemes, including the imminent death of my father, will be released to the commission."

He walks towards the gun until the barrel is against his head.

"They'd kill you before the next sunset."

He's a madman.

I try to back up and out the door during their standoff, but a wall of muscle quickly stops me. Two guards stare down at me and dare me to move."

My father tilts his head and lightly squeezes the trigger, laughing when the hollow click of an empty chamber sounds. Leo doesn't react at all.

My father uncocks the gun and puts it away in his suit jacket like a favorite pen and shrugs before saying, "Another time then."

He walks to his bar and pours a drink. He eyes me with derision before commanding Leo and his guards.

"Take her. The auction begins in four hours."

My flailing arms and blood-curdling scream are cut off by a familiar prick to my neck.

Damn. Not Again.

23

ROCCO

"How the hell did you miss this? Aren't you supposed to be the boy genius? The aloof fucker that keeps us safe?!"

The feel of bone breaking beneath my fist is music to my ears. It replaces the endless buzzing that's plagued me since the moment I allowed Lucia to step off the Santa Anna. I know breaking Enzo's nose won't carry me to Lucia any quicker, but it sure as hell makes me feel better. It's something to do until our contact give us the clear to fuck up Matteo Ricci and Leo's entire world.

"What the fuck is wrong with you Rocco! You broke my nose! You're paying to get it fixed!"

Enzo holds his crooked nose between his thumb and index finger as the blood continues to pour from his nostrils. The scene of his crushed flesh and flowing blood is like a red flag to a bull, and I'm ready to charge.

I can't believe he dares to tell me I'm paying for his

crushed cartilage; when my wife is God knows where with a madman because of his fuck up!

I'll kill him.

I lunge, but I'm pulled back with a harsh jerk. I turn to punch whoever has the gall to touch me, but pause when I see it's Mario in his fighter's stance. He's ready for battle, and although I can take him, I won't walk away unscathed like I would with Enzo.

Enzo can hold his own, but he doesn't spend enough time in the gym or the ring, so he's a lightweight compared to me. Besides that, Enzo is the weird type who thrives on pain and doesn't mind taking a punch. He wouldn't even think of hitting me back.

Mario, on the other hand, is as dedicated to boxing and Krav Maga as I am. We're an even match, and if it comes to it, he won't pull any punches. I can't afford to nurse an injury while planning the most important rescue mission of my life.

"Mario, I know that's your brother, but I'm his boss. If he needs to be fucked up then that's what's going to happen. He gave us valuable information thirty minutes too late, and now my wife is in the clutches of Matteo Ricci and my sadistic cousin. That can't go unpunished."

Mario exhales and crosses his arms. "Rocco, this is as much your fault as it is Enzo's. Even more so. It's your pride that got your wife stolen from under your nose."

I see red.

I punch Mario across the jaw. His head turns with the impact, but his hands are quick as lightning. He returns a heavy punch to my face and two to the gut. When I wrap my arms around him, we both tumble to the ground.

"Get up!" I hear a hoarse but strong voice through my violent haze. "Both of you, get the fuck up!"

I glance towards the door as I fight Mario off and see my uncle pointing at us. I give Mario a stiff elbow to the side, and he looks towards the door. When he sees the don, he lets me go with a curse and scrambles to his feet. When he reaches his hand down to help me, I shoot a glare in his direction as we lock hands.

My uncle has made quite the recovery. Four days ago, his home was blown up with him inside it. He sustained a head injury and some shrapnel in his leg. The fact that the man is talking to us as he leans on his cane is a testament to his strength. I see the pain edging at the corners of his eyes, but he ignores it. He remains the leader of our family, and he will rule with an iron fist until the day he dies.

He falls into a nearby chair and eyes us with disgust. "There's no time for this. According to my sources, Lucia is on the east side of Manhattan at one of Matteo's residences."

I shoot a look at Enzo, and he nods. He knows he has about as much time as my uncle's lecture to map out that home so that we can go.

"By now, I'm sure she's met my ruthless son and is scared shitless. It won't take very long for Matteo to get your marriage annulled and her tied to Leo or someone worse. You kidnapped her, and neither the commission, the church, or the law will respect it if that is brought to light."

I shake my head. "She'll never agree to that. Lucia won't sign another marriage certificate or submit her body to another man. She'd die first."

Uncle Thomasso slowly shakes his head. "That's what

I'm afraid of. She's headstrong, and those two stronzos will break her. Time is not on your side. What's the plan? Why aren't you already in your cars?"

"We're leaving as soon as Enzo maps out Matteo's Oak Park home and his two southside clubs," Mario says. "He's remotely disarming security at all three locations just in case he moves her. Matteo cut off all communication with us, and we can't seem to track Lucia's phone."

My uncle snorts. "He probably confiscated and destroyed it the moment he got her off that boat."

I nod. "Mario, Enzo, and I will divide and lead three strike teams. It should be a quick and bloody hit. We're leaving no prisoners."

Uncle Thomasso pulls a cigar from his pocket, and Mario immediately steps in to light it. After a few puffs, he speaks.

"Sounds straightforward enough, but he knows you're coming. You need to move quickly and reach him before he sells Lucia to the highest bidder. That's all she is to him now, a payday, and a tarnished one at that. Honestly, that's all she ever was to him."

I narrow my eyes at my uncle; he's talking in riddles. What bidder is he talking about? According to our intel, he's given her to Leo, choosing to align himself with that fool instead of the actual head of our family. However, now my uncle talks of something else entirely. He's hiding something."

I move closer to him. "What aren't you telling me, Uncle?"

Casually, he takes a puff from his cigar, and it takes an act of God for me not to snatch it out of his mouth and shake the same sense of urgency he says we need into him. He must not know that I'm two seconds from losing my mind and not giving a damn who he or anyone else is in this organization. My beautiful, innocent wife is somewhere scared and in danger, all because of me.

This would never have happened if I had just told her the truth from the beginning. Truth would have been the best protection from all of this, even if that protection extended to me. I'd rather not have her and have her be safe than live through the hell of our current situation. I tried to keep her for myself, and now she's with the devil.

My uncle chokes on a puff of smoke and continues. "That night, when you brought me the pictures of Lucia and her mother, I was shocked. Not because I didn't know that Matteo had a daughter. I was surprised because no one was ever able to figure out who or where she was."

"Wait!" I jab my finger at my uncle's face. When he glares at me, I stand my ground. "What do you mean you knew he had a daughter? How? And why did you act like you didn't know that day I came to your office?"

My uncle chuckles and shrugs, between his nonchalance and the constant clicking of keys from Enzo at my desk. I swear I'm having a nervous breakdown.

"You young boys think you're so smart with your smartphones and tracking systems. Your video cameras and GPS devices watch you as much as you watch them. What good has it gotten you in this situation? Your wife is in the clutches of two of the most despicable men ever to walk the earth. You obsessively tracked her and lost her. Back in my day, everything was about relationships. It's people, stupid! The best surveillance you can ever have is the person who feeds your subject and washes his shit-stained drawers."

I rub my face, sigh, and fall into the chair across from him. "Uncle, please just tell us what you know."

"That's what I was doing before you interrupted me, now may I finish?"

St. Peter, St. Linus, St. Anacletus, St. Clement I...

My uncle smirks as I whisper the Pope's in order. He wanted this rise out of me. But why?

"As I was saying, Matteo's cook is a plant. His celebrated chef is my third cousin from the old country, and he has no idea. She's cooked for that man for over twenty years and fed me information when I needed it. She knew he had the daughter, but she never could get any Intel on who she was. So, when you came to me, I thought it was the perfect opportunity. We could get that bastard's daughter and marry her off to you. Then she would forever be under our control."

I knew the plans he had for her. He never wanted to marry her to Leo, well, not specifically. It's about her being pawned off to whichever family will pay the most to have her. Matteo has no other heirs, so upon his death, everything will pass to her. But the selfish, controlling bastard wanted to make the match something that benefited him. He sent her that money monthly to keep her until he was ready to take her himself. He doesn't care if she goes to an Armenian or Russian; he wants more money and a way to take us down."

"Your uncle's right." Enzo rushes over, out of breath and wheezing. "I finally tapped into all the security cameras and placed dummy feeds into all of them. I was also able to listen to one of the bugs the cook planted in the kitchen for us a few years ago."

"The fuck! You knew about the cook and Matteo's house! Why didn't you tell me?"

Enzo cuts his eyes at my uncle to get permission to speak. My uncle nods.

"Yes, I always knew. Your uncle wouldn't let me tell you because he said the fewer people who knew about her, the safer she would be. He wouldn't even let me tell you tonight."

My uncle pipes up, taking the cigar out of his mouth for a blessed minute.

"That's because I wanted to make sure you loved the lamb. Lucia is a good girl, and I'd rescue her and keep her safe from you if I thought you'd hurt her. But seeing how crazy you are over her, I know you need to be the one to go and get her."

Enzo shakes his head. "None of that matters now. What matters is they're planning an auction to sell Lucia off within the next three hours. Matteo set the auction in his basement. His cook tells me he's drugged her and chained her in some cage."

I let out a roar of anguish as I punched a few holes into a nearby wall. I'm unleashed, and I know I won't be satisfied until every drop of blood from any man who touched my wife is pooling around their dead bodies.

"What else?" I yell.

Enzo continues. "According to the guest list I was able to wrestle from a friend, the Armenians, Russians, and even the Irish are coming to bid on her. It seems instead of keeping her bride price high for virginity, he's driving up the price by letting all our enemies know she was once your wife. A wife that you loved. He's promised they can do anything to her once they have her."

I nod. "We must go right now. There's not a moment to lose."

Mario stops me as I charge towards the door. "Wait, Rocco, we can't go in there half-cocked. We need more manpower to stop an auction with that many heads of families and their guards. It will take more than the three of us and our soldiers."

I shake my head. "I don't care what you think, Mario. I'm not waiting any longer. My wife is in danger and none of those motherfuckers are laying a finger on her. Do you hear me, not one." I growl.

Mario looks me in the eye and squeezes my shoulders. "I know, brother, she's important to me too. Aria thinks the world of her. I've never seen you at peace until she came into your life, and we're going to get her back. But we'll do it in a way that keeps her and all of us alive. Capiche?"

My breaths come hard, but they finally slow down. "OK, what's the plan?"

Mario laughs. Oh, it's the same plan. We're going to crash their party, smash some heads, and grab your wife. We need a few more men to help. Give me two minutes and we're on our way."

I stomp away. "Fine, meet me in the armored G wagon. You have 119 seconds or I'm leaving without you."

24

LUCIA

Life moves fast.

One minute, I was in my father's dining room watching him point a gun at Leonardo Romano.

I was reeling, but in firm control of my faculties.

Then there came the infamous poke.

I really hate needles.

Now, I'm oiled up and wearing a gold sequined bikini, chained inside a cage placed on some sort of stage. My head is killing me, and my throat feels like it's on fire.

The make-up they put on me is so heavy that I can feel it pressing into my skin. My coveted curls are fried and ironed into a straight sheet of hair hanging down my back. The only position my chains comfortably allow is kneeling, and the stilettos on my feet are digging into the back of my thighs. I could stand up if I had the energy, but it would be painful, and from the length, I would only be able to face forward.

I hear murmurs, but I have no idea who's making the sounds. There's an audience, but for what?

Then I remember my father saying something about an auction and a high bride price. I shiver, recalling the cold calculation of his voice.

Truly, he can't mean to sell his child?

The murmurs get louder, and whatever small crowd is gathered is restless.

"Alright, men, settle down. You'll all get a chance to bid on my lovely daughter."

My father's mirth is unsettling. *The bastard's having fun.*

With great effort, I turn my neck to peek behind me. Leo stands there with a deadly grin on his face. He winks at me and I almost puke. He's playing babysitter while my father plays the gracious host. I turn back to the sound of my father's voice as he continues to calm the crow. It's clear he's hosted an event like this before; he's in his element.

What sounds like a gavel hits the podium. "Now let's start the bidding at $500,000."

"Wait! I want to fuck the whore first. Make sure she's worth my time. Let's at least strip her to see the assets." A Spanish accent answers in protest. Then he approaches the stage and gets close enough to be in my line of sight. He's at least fifty years old and wearing a hideous suit made out of what I assume is the Mexican Cartel's flag. My father whispers something in his ear, and the cartel leader laughs before backing off. He was promised something that appeased him.

This is hell.

I once thought my husband's basement was hell. But right now, I'd give anything to be back in that dark, cool space...alone. I'd even prefer to be laid across his lap waiting for his firm and gentle hand to land on my ass; as I silently beg him to punish me for being naughty. Then he'd kiss me for being his good girl.

His wife.

Rocco lied to me, but he kept me safe. He never made me feel cheap or unwanted. Instead, he put me on a pedestal of his creation. I sat so high above the world and its tragedies that my new reality only had pleasure and peace.

Even if he is an overbearing, overprotective, and controlling jerk.

He's mine.

I feel guilty because I can't hate him even if sanity demands that I should. Rocco snatched me, kicking and screaming, from my life. I didn't love my life, but it was good enough. I spent every day playing the piano and reaping a professional harvest from all my labor. That's all I thought I had the right to ask for.

Then Rocco came and expanded the borders of my desire by making me fall in love with him on that damn mountain in Italy.

Now I need him.

I would have been taken from my life, one way or the other, but at least with a monster like Leo, I would have known what I was getting from the start and never tossed my heart into the ring.

The two men who should care for me the most have lied to me. Their cruelty is harsher than that filthy man calling me a whore. They called me their princess and queen, only to both use me as a bargaining chip in their violent aspirations.

If I ever get out of here, and I hope I do, I'll know to keep my heart in my chest, locked behind self-preservation, caution, and restraint.

Because I know Rocco is coming for me. At least I pray he is.

I could never trust him as my husband again, but I damn sure can trust him to get me out of this cage.

Does he even know I'm here? By now, he has to know. Enzo can track me, right? My phone was taken, but there's got to be some hidden microchip in my skin or something.

Lord knows, Rocco and Mario drugged me enough to get it done. That's how all the mafia romances on my Kindle end: with the hero miraculously tracking down the heroine against all logical odds.

Except, this is not a story. This is my life, and right now, a bright light is shining on me so harshly I can't see a foot in front of me. *I'm fucked.*

The unmistakable boom of a gun shakes me from my despair. Then another. The spotlight shining in my face cuts off, and I welcome the darkness as I hear the scuffles and screams of men.

Loud gunshots echo around the room. I scramble to get to my feet, but it makes no difference. I'm still kneeling and chained inside this cage. I shiver in the pitch-black room. It sounds like the world is ending around me.

25

ROCCO

The G-Wagon screeches to a halt in front of Matteo Ricci's Manhattan fortress, and I'm out before the engine finishes dying.

We had eyes and ears inside through a small, remote drone that Enzo managed together. The last thing I heard before we arrived was that cartel bastard calling my world a whore.

He's dying first.

There are guards at Matteo's door. We expected that, and immediately, gunfire erupts like thunder around me.

The sharp, acrid scent of cordite and copper blood slams into my senses—metallic, thick, and familiar as breath. I inhale it like oxygen, like war. I push forward with a fury I don't bother to contain.

Behind me, my army of one hundred fans is out, a black wave of death cresting against the manicured estate. Each man bears the Roman crest across his chest. Each man was forged by loyalty, hardened by loss, and baptized by the promise I made when they touched my ring.

They came for blood.

I came for her.

This isn't a rescue.

It's an eradication.

I lead the charge, eyes cold, heart burning. We breach the doors, and hell follows us in.

By the time I enter behind my men, the auction room is chaos incarnate—gilded chandeliers swinging wildly, smoke curling in tendrils across the velvet-draped ceiling, men screaming over the cacophony of bullets and death. Ricci's men, the cartel muscle—they're caught off guard. They die screaming.

A body charges me from the side. I barely glance before my knife finds his throat—a geyser of blood arcs through the air. I step over the twitching corpse like it's nothing because it is.

None of them matter.

Only one face lives in my mind. Only one heartbeat calls to me through this madness.

Lucia.

I scan the chaos—firing, killing, moving—and then I see her.

On stage.

Spotlighted. Bound.

A gold bikini clings to her like sin. Her ankles are shackled. Her wrists were bruised. There's a collar around her neck like she's some fucking possession.

A guttural snarl tears from my chest.

She looks like a fucking offering.

Like prey.

Like bait for the highest bidder.

A man dares to place his hand on her thigh as she trembles.

Not my wife.

I raise my Glock and shoot him between the eyes. His blood paints the curtain behind her. Her scream chokes off, her eyes flaring wide—and they find me.

I guess he had to die first.

Even in the chaos. Even in the blood.

Lucia sees me.

Her breath stutters. Her lips part.

She sees what I've become for her.

What I've done.

What I will still do.

Every part of me is soaked in vengeance. Every heartbeat drums her name. My hands, my soul, my sins—they belong to her.

I motion sharply, and Mario breaks from my side.

"Get her," I bark. "Now. Kill anyone who looks at her wrong."

He nods, already moving, slicing his way through bodies like a blade through butter.

I head left, toward the cartel VIPs still seated, surrounded by my soldiers. Each one has a knife to his throat, a gun to his temple. They think we'll negotiate.

They think wrong.

And then I see him—the bastard who spat her name with

filth on his tongue. The cartel leader has too much money and not enough fear. The man who called my wife a whore.

He's grinning. *Grinning.*

I cross the space in three strides, knock aside the soldier holding him, and drag the fucker to his knees by the back of his neck.

"No one calls her that," I growl.

He tries to speak. I don't let him.

I draw my machete from its sheath at my back and, in one smooth swing, take his head clean off.

Blood spurts high, a crimson fountain soaking the floor and the silk drapes.

Gasps ripple through the survivors.

No one speaks. No one moves.

Only Lucia. Her breath hitches. Her eyes—glassy, stunned, full of horror and relief and love—watch as I stand over the corpse of the man who defiled her with his words.

I've only just begun.

26

I hear Rocco's fury before I lay eyes on him.

He's out there somewhere. Beyond the smoke and chaos, I hear the battle cries of men fighting and dying.

And I know that's my angel of death delivering retribution.

When I see Rocco, my heart damn near stops.

We lock eyes, but he doesn't run to me as I'd expect. Instead, he pulls a huge knife from the back of his tactical pants and whispers something in Mario's ear, never taking his eyes off of me.

Why isn't he coming? Is he mad that I left?

Then I see it. The garrish man draped in the Mexican Cartel's colors who called me a whore. Rocco slices his head clean off, and the bastard's blood washes the walls.

My eyes never leave his and I'm wet as fuck.

I'm going to need therapy after this.

Then I feel a tug on my ankle, and I jerk at the touch.

Someone's in here with me!

I am frozen in terror as I imagine one of those drooling men taking me away. My worst nightmare is confirmed when the waist grabs me.

"I'm going to get us out of here and I'm going to take you back home and fuck you until you can't move." He snatches my ankle.

"I don't know where your dad ran off to, but he stupidly left me with the key to this," he says as he frantically unshackles me. "He and my father think they're so smart. They think they can control me and the world around them. But I'll show all these older men who the real boss is. He snatches my hair. "Come on bitch."

I shudder at the sound of Leo's gravelly voice. When I'm freed from the cage and in the darkness behind the cage, he drags me down to the floor and his coarse hands slide down my ass, thighs, and legs.

Something snaps in me, and I try to kick him away. I need to get off this stage to freedom.

To Rocco.

But Leo is too strong. He grabs my legs and pulls me close to him. He regains control of my waist and grips me tightly. That's when I feel the hard metal barrel of a nine millimeter against my temple.

"Calm down," he purrs. "I just want to take you home with me, but I might have to change my plans if you're not going to cooperate." Leo gets to his feet and pulls me up with him. He shoves the gun into my back and slides his forearm and bicep around my neck as he forces me deeper backstage.

Without warning, the lights turn on, and I'm blinded as

my eyes adjust. Leo jumps down sideways off the stage before dragging me toward the back of the room.

I choke as his grip tightens around my neck. I blink tears out of my eyes and see Mario dressed in all black striding forcefully toward us cocking a giant shotgun. He looks every bit the part of a cold-blooded Mafia hitman.

"Leo! Let her go!"

Leo cocks the gun at my temple. "Give me one reason why I shouldn't blow her head off right now."

Mario smirks. "Come on. The game is over. You've lost. You can leave here alive, or you can leave in a box. Let the girl go."

Leo scoffs, his eyes are wild as he presses the gun into my head. "Rocco doesn't deserve her; she's my birthright. The don is my dad, not his! I'm the heir. I'm the king, and the king gets the queen!" He screeches.

I think I'm going to pass out. *I don't want to die here.*

"You've got nowhere to run, Leo." Leo turns, and we are greeted by Enzo walking up behind him. As he turns, I feel Leo's grip loosen. I jerk free from him with all my strength and manage to get free. All I hear is gunfire as I fall to the floor and black out.

I am brought back to consciousness by a blanket being thrown over my shoulders as Mario cradles me in his arms. A few feet away from me, Leo is lying out in a pool of blood with a gigantic bloody hole in his chest.

I thought Rocco would be the one to kill him.

I'm shocked at how overjoyed I am that he's dead.

Good Riddance.

Mario gestures for me to sit down and stay quiet. I obey.

My eyes seek out my husband and I find him across the room, splattered with blood, standing over the headless corpse of the cartel leader who called me a whore.

Eight men are sitting in chairs facing the stage, and about fifty men surround them. Each seated man has a gun trained on him and an armed man with a knife to his throat.

It feels like nobody's breathing except Rocco. My eyes dart around the room, and my father is nowhere to be seen. That worries me.

"So you all thought that you would disgrace my wife and get away with it?" His smile is deadly.

You're all high-ranking men in your organizations; you should know better than that."

"Did you think that you would come into this stronzo's basement and take what's mine!"

His voice is unhinged, and so am I. Hearing him claim me so decidedly is making my pussy weep, and this is not the time for that.

There's something about seeing those same $2000 black Italian shoes that came that first night to take me from his dungeon, standing in the spilled blood of our enemy, that makes me want to jump his bones.

God, I need help.

Another man, this one with a Russian accent, dares to speak. "Fieri, we didn't know she was yours. Her father brought us here under pretenses. We thought this was an honest sale."

Rocco nods his head at the guard standing in front of the Russian, and immediately, the sound of a gunshot echoes through the room. It is followed by a cloud of red mist and the blood-curdling screams of the Bratva leader, as he clutches his knee.

"Fuuuucccck," The man howls. Tears roll down his face. The scene would be comical if it weren't so tragic, terrifying, and honest.

Rocco walks around and eyes each man. But he doesn't look at me, and I feel cold.

"Now, does anybody else want to lie to me? You all have two kneecaps a piece, and I'd be happy to oblige."

No one makes a sound.

Rocco gestures to the dead man on the floor as he strolls around the room. "As much as you all make me sick, I am inclined to let you live. The Don would prefer to avoid all-out war even as I avenge my wife. As you all can see, we may already have some nasty repercussions from the Cartel, but we'll handle that with no problems." Rocco shrugs and twirls his gun.

"You all know that the Romano's don't stand for the trafficking or selling of women, and you dare to do this here? With my wife?! You must have forgotten Chicago is Romano territory! Ricci is no more consequential than a squirrel trying to get a nut. When I find him, he's dead!"

Where the fuck is my father?

"This is what's going to happen. You will each be escorted into waiting vehicles. Unfortunately, your bodyguards have been disposed of, so you're under our protection, and as we all know, you must pay for protection. When you get home, you will notice we've removed a small tribute from your financial accounts. Just enough to repay me, my wife, and my family for your lack of good judgment. I hope you'll remember our generosity tonight. If not, the Romano's will slowly drain every asset you own until the Don is satisfied. Just remember, we have control of your financial accounts until we feel you have sufficiently learned your lesson. You can't buy a pack of gum unless we allow it."

He walks over and spits on the dead man who dared to call me a whore. "Burn this one and send his ashes to his witless son and widow. Let them know that I send my regards. Get the rest of them out of here before my patience runs out."

When every man has left, Rocco drops his gun and dismisses Mario. "Go find Matteo." Mario runs off, and then it's just Rocco and me.

He runs to me and throws the blanket off my body. Frantically, he touches every inch of me like he's scared I'll disappear in front of his eyes."

"Are you OK? Did anyone touch you? I should have killed that fucker Leo myself!"

The tears in his eyes are unsettling. I stroked his face to calm him down. "Shhh, I'm fine, Rocco. No one touched me, you got here just in time. You always come when I need you, even before I realize it. Thank You.

He scoffs and turns his head. "Don't thank me. This is all my fault. I should never have lied to you, and I should have done everything in my power to keep you safely on that boat with me. I just felt like I had to prove to myself that I could let you go. That you were just a pawn."

I sniffle, remembering the way he just let me go. Every few steps, I kept looking back, expecting him to follow me and drag me back on the boat. But he didn't. That's when I knew he meant more to me than I meant to him. I love him and hate him at the same damn time.

He slips his fingers under my chin and forces my eyes up to his. "But you know what, Lucia?"

"What," I whisper.

"You aren't just a pawn. You're my queen, my wife, la mia piccola palla di fuoco. I love you more than anything. I'd burn down this entire world for you if you asked."

"Would you?" I run my fingers through his thick hair and drown in his icy blue stare.

He laughs. "I have already come very close. Those men represent the heads of the eight largest crime organizations in this city. The man I killed was the head of the Mexican Cartel, so our dealings with them are not finished. Your father is also on the run, and I won't rest until I've killed the coward. Those men will be compliant for a while because we have them by the balls. What I did tonight probably made my uncle the most powerful man in the underworld. But this type of power does not come without a price. Soon, the Russians, Armenians, and even the Triads will want blood."

"So... you went to war just for me?"

He nods and pulls me close. "And I'd do it again in a heartbeat. Forgive me, Lucia. I will never lie to you again. If you want to annul our marriage, I understand. Maybe we can find a way for you to perform again. You will always need security, but I can make anything happen for you. I can't live without you. Give me a chance to show you how good I can be."

I pause. *Isn't this what I wanted?* To be free of this forced vow and restart my career? Now that he's offering it to me, I realize that's not my life anymore. He is.

I shake my head. "No. I am the daughter of Don Matteo Ricci and the wife of the Romano family's consigliere. My life is full of danger, but it's also full of love. Together, we will take my father down and take down what's left of his kingdom. I love you, Rocco Fieri, and you can't get rid of me that easily."

"Never," he growls while he wraps his arms around me and takes me into a deep kiss.

As he reclaims me, I think back on how much my life has changed since this man kidnapped me. Joy wraps around my heart as I realize my life didn't end when Rocco Fieri chained me in his basement.

That's when my life truly began.

THE END

Thank You for Reading "One Savage Union" If you loved reading this #HappyBlackRomance as much as I did writing it, please leave a review on Amazon or Goodreads.

Amazon

GoodReads

Mario's Story is next! Stay tuned and follow me on TikTok to catch this Winter's release date.

Or....

Are you on My Mailing List? Stay current on all my future releases, and join my ARC Team!

Join Mailing List

EPILOGUE

LUCIA

ONE MONTH LATER...

White Lilies blanket every inch of Duomo di Ravello's ceiling and walls. It's my wedding day, and the historic church at Ravello's center never smelled so sweet. The flowers' scent calms me, and their beautiful petals delight me as I walk into my future. The lily is Italy's national flower, and Rocco insisted that our Amalfi wedding pay tribute to it, as he also likes the purity it represents.

To him, my innocence redeems his sins, but I know better. Only God can judge us and forgive our sins. I'm no deity, but if it makes him sleep better at night, I'll be anything he needs.

Walking down this aisle with Uncle Thomasso at my side is unreal. The older man is still injured from the blast at his house a month ago and he's using a cane. Regardless, he's walking tall, and proud as a peacock.

He's insisted I call him uncle now that he and I are truly becoming husband and wife in front of the holy virgin. I've learned that deep down, the Romano Don is a sweet, older man who values blood above all else. I'm honored he asked to walk me down the aisle since I'm practically an orphan.

A small spray of sadness washes over me when I think about how my mother never got to see me in this wedding dress. It's a simple satin sheath of ivory that fits me like a second skin. The front is cut into a low V-neck with spaghetti straps of real diamonds holding it to my body. The train of the dress is approximately six feet long and the back of my dress cuts so low, you almost get a peek at my ass. It's sexy and elegant, and my Ghanaian mother would have clucked her tongue in chastisement before kissing me with pride. She died way too soon. Chrisette Asare would have fussed that this was all too much while secretly loving the fanfare.

My father is on the run from my husband and uncle Thomasso for trying to kill them and subsequently selling me to the highest bidder. Instead of having a loving father to give me away on one of the most important days of my life, I only have the memory of a monster. It's hard to feel completely safe while he's still free in the world.

When I look up and see Rocco's twinkling eyes, I know all that doesn't matter. He stands alone because I had no one to stand at my side. My happiness and safety are encompassed inside this 6'4 man standing in a Black Armani Tuxedo with the air of a Greek God. He's my savior. The man who kidnapped me and took my body for his pleasure before spilling blood for me is no saint. But he's all mine. His penetrating gaze commands my joy and promises to do everything in his power to bring it to me.

Like a good girl, I obey and smile. It's time to enjoy the spoils of war.

"Benvenuta in famiglia, bella," Uncle Thomasso murmurs before placing my hand in Rocco's at the top of the altar. My Italian is improving, and I can pick out the words 'welcome' and 'beautiful'. I smile and kiss him on the cheek before my possessive fiancée jerks away my hand.

I look into Rocco's eyes and smirk before whispering, "You can't seriously be jealous of your uncle, Rocco."

He chuckles before leaning over and biting my earlobe. It causes me to gasp, and the priest gives us a warning look. I should have worn a veil.

"I'm not jealous piccola ragazza, I'm cautious. You think he's a gentle older man, but I've seen him charm the pants off women more than half his age. Plus, no one gets your smile, touch, or kiss but me." He growls possessively, and my stupid heart loves it.

The ceremony is condensed from the standard 60-minute Catholic Mass to a 20-minute exchange of vows. Rocco goes first and mixes up the order of things. Placing a five-carat infinity band on my finger first, he kisses my hand and then recites his love for me.

"La mia bellissima piccola palla di fuoco. You alone changed the trajectory of my life. I thought my ascension inside the Sicilian mafia was what life was all about until I took one look into your eyes. That's when I knew that I'd throw it all away to own your heart. You are the most important thing to me, and I don't have the words to explain how much you are the bone of my bone and flesh of my flesh. Thankfully, an author by the name of Charlotte Brontë had her hero say the words to her infamous heroine, Jane Eyre, when he thought he'd lost her, and yet she returned. When I let you walk off that boat, I knew his pain. When I rescued you and had you back in my arms, I thought it was only a dream to be so happy and complete. The few days without you were hell, but the forever days before us will be heaven. Bronte's written words are what I shall recite tonight..."

> ...there is enchantment in the very hour I am now spending with you. Who can tell what a dark, dreary, hopeless life I have dragged on for [years] past? Doing nothing, expecting nothing; merging night in day; feeling but the sensation of cold when I let the fire go out, of hunger when I forgot to eat: and then a ceaseless sorrow, and, at times, a very delirium of desire to behold my Lucia again.

"I'll never fail you again. I love you. Ti amerò sempre (I'll always love you).

His words bring tears to my eyes and dance within my heart. My hand cups his cheek as I take his lips in a soft kiss. We linger, lips locked, until the priest clears his throat in reprimand. Rocco shoots him a look of death while I hold back tears of joy and laughter. Once all is calm, I touch Rocco's arm and nod that I'm ready to recite my vows to him.

Slowly, I slip the 3-carat Black titanium and black diamond David Yurman wedding band onto his ring finger and begin.

"I'm afraid I have no literary words to recite tonight. But I think that's OK. What I do have is a true declaration of my devotion to you and your family. You are my heart and human form, and before you, I was not living; I only survived. Half a life is better than no life at all, but a full life is God's greatest blessing. Thank you. Sei il grande amore della mia vita (you are the love of my life)."

Rocco grabs me by my waist and pulls me indecently close before devouring me in a soul-stealing kiss. Our priest finally gives up any pretense of decorum and announces us man and wife. I faintly hear the cheers in the background because all I can focus on is the buzzing of pleasure in my ears. My husband's tongue is claiming every inch of my mouth while his hands squeeze my ass and his dick presses hard into my belly. It's a filthy kiss, and I love it.

When we come up for air, he groans in my ear.

"I need to be inside of you right now, or I'll burst. I know just the place, come."

Rocco takes my hand and practically drags me down the aisle as well-wishers clap and throw flower petals at our retreating form. When we're in the vestibule, he pauses to consider which way he should go, and then he turns right towards the dressing room I used.

Once inside the room, Rocco slams the door and presses me against it so that my ass faces him. I turn my head to the side and breathe heavily through my arousal and excitement. I feel his tongue stroke from the top of my ass up my entire back.

'Fuck Lucia, this dress is sexy as hell. I don't know whether to fuck you with gratitude for wearing it for me or if I should punish you for teasing me and every other man in this church with this ass."

Quickly, he lands two slaps to each of my ass cheeks, and I moan.

Feeling cocky, I tease him and rub my ass over his growing cock. "I think a little of both is on order."

He chuckles and spins me around." It's too bad I must share you with the world for a few more hours, and I can't rip you out of this dress to make my pussy come. So, instead, punishment will have to be imposed. You'll be wet and wanting for me the entire reception. That will teach you not to wear inaccessible clothing when I'm this hot for you, on your knees, my little ball of fire. It's time to suck your husband's cock."

I turn around and immediately drop to my knees. Looking up at him; I open my mouth wide and wait for his cock to fill me. He gently rubs my cheek with one hand while he unzips his pants with the other.

"Baby, you look so beautiful waiting for my cock like this. I'll reward you tonight if you take daddy's cock like a good girl and swallow every drop. I'd hate to get cum on your pretty dress. That would be quite the show for our guests."

I nod and stick my tongue out. I honestly don't give a damn if the world sees his cum on me, I like being marked by him.

Rocco grabs the back of my head, pushing hairpins into my scalp. My intricate updo is ruined, but I don't care. The pain turns me on even more.

"I won't be gentle." He warns.

You never are...

In one sharp thrust he slams his dick into my mouth and slides it down my throat. I've learned to relax my gag reflex with Rocco, and I'm rewarded with his grunt of pleasure as my nose hits his abdomen."

"Of fuck, wife, damn that feels so good. You take your husband's cock so well."

He slides out to give me a moment to breathe before slamming in again and tightening his grip in my hair." That's it Lucia, let daddy fuck this pretty mouth."

His dirty words turn me on, and even though I can't get to my pussy in this tight ass dress, my girl is working overtime getting herself off. When he pulls out of me and takes my face in both hands, I know what's coming.

With hard and swift strokes, he fucks my mouth like he wishes he could fuck my pussy. The intensity makes me moan and come right there on my knees. My eyes roll back in pleasure, and Rocco notices..

"Fuck! Baby, did you just come without any manual stimulation? Damn...." His roar fills the room and ropes of cum jet down my throat. I swallow every drop like a good girl, and when he's squeezed his last drop out, he collapses and leans forward onto the door behind my head.

I pop his dick out my mouth and lick my fingers clean. " How'd I do?"

He looks down at me and releases a harsh laugh before bending down to kiss my forehead." You're fucking incredible Lucia. Come on, let's get you cleaned up before the cavalry comes looking for us."

It takes us a few minutes, but we both take the time to get ourselves in a presentable state before opening the door.

When we step out of the room, we hear a slap and the high-pitched scream of a woman. When we turn around, we see Mario being assaulted by a beautiful slip of a woman. Seeing the small siren with more hair than body attack Mario's massive and sturdy 6'5 frame makes me giggle.

"I hate you, get off me! sei un fottuto stronzo."

When she verbally assaults him, I tense. "Not many people get away with calling Mario Bianchi a fucking asshole."

"Just calm down, Daniella, and stop hitting me, or you won't like your punishment."

"Fuck you! She spits." *The girl's got guts.*

Then a familiar scene plays out in front of me when I see Mario turn her back to his front and quickly press a needle behind her ear. He kisses her gently and mumbles sorry before turning to look at us.

My mouth is agape, but Rocco doesn't look surprised at all. *What in the actual fuck.* I try to slip my hand away, but Rocco squeezes me tighter before he addresses Mario.

"Is that the whore you almost missed my wedding for?" Rocco seethes.

I was wondering why I saw him sitting in the back.

Mario's lips are thin. "Don't call her that ever again unless you'd like your wedding and funeral on the same day."

Rocco chuckles, but I don't see what's so funny.

"Who is that girl, Mario, and why are you drugging her?" I demand.

And how much of that drug do they have lying around?

He doesn't answer me at first. Mario and I have never been the best of friends. From the very beginning, when he kidnapped me from my apartment, our relationship has been tenuous at best.

When I married his best friend, he became cordial, but I never got the feeling he liked me very much. By duty, he has to show me more than just a modicum of respect. His eyes slide over to Rocco, asking permission to speak. Rocco nods, and Mario takes a deep breath.

"When we rescued you from your father's home, we found more cells in the basement of his house. All of them were empty except for one; unfortunately, he had already moved most of his product."

The way Mario says product with disgust doesn't escape me. My body trembles with the realization that he's talking about innocent women. Rocco moves his arm around my waist and steadies me with a kiss. I'm relieved to know Rocco's family does not believe in the trafficking of women like my father does. Taking a deep breath, I nod for Mario to continue.

"When I was looking for your father to make sure he wasn't hiding anywhere in the house, I found a hidden door behind one of the cells and heard a woman's whimper and screams for help."

He pauses to look down at the beautiful woman, with cascading auburn hair, in his arms with...emotion. Something I didn't even think Mario Bianchi had, but it's clear that he cares about her.

"This is Daniella McClanahan. She is the daughter of the

now-deceased Daniel McClanahan, former head of the Irish mob. The Bratva took her and gave her to your father two months ago. Your father was supposed to watch her until the Bratva finished decimating her clan. Her virginity and stature would go for a high price on the underground market."

Disgusting. That plan sounds way too close to home. What is the fascination these old mobsters have with women and their virginity?

Rocco squeezes me tight and fills in the rest of the blanks. "Your father wanted her for himself and hid her. The Bratva didn't know that he planned never to give her back. He hoped they would take a fancy to you and trade with you. He'd already started violating the girl. If the Bratva knew, they would have killed him."

Do they know now?" I ask breathlessly.

Rocco nods. "Yes, and they want his head on a silver platter. But they also want the girl. She holds the keys to half her father's fortune, and instead of selling her, they want to marry her off to their Pakhan. A sixty-year-old man who will use and break her. He's known for his viciousness. He's buried three wives already."

I gasp, and a tear falls. " We have to help her."

Rocco sighs. "I wish it were that simple. As I've told Mario, your rescue cost us. If we take this girl, it will most certainly mean war."

I look at my husband and squeeze his waist. " But we have to do something!"

His eyes soften, and I know I've got him. Mario interrupts.

"Don't worry, Lucia. I'm never giving her up; she's mine.

I'll kill anyone who tries to take her. Il mio gattina's claws are out, and she does not understand her predicament. But she will learn."

I smile at his pet name for her—h*is kitten.*

He nods at Rocco, and he holds her closer to his chest before marching off.

Seeing his resolve to keep her safe calms me. Mario will protect her with his life, and God help the men who try to take away his pet.

ALSO BY LOUISE LENNOX

ALSO BY LOUISE LENNOX

THE SEXY SOVEREIGN SERIES (ALSO ON AUDIBLE)

Craving a King: https://geni.us/CravingAKing

Choosing the Chief: https://geni.us/AdomandMaya

Possessing A Prince: https://geni.us/SenyandAbena

THE KIAWAH KISSES SERIES

Merry Kiss Me : https://geni.us/Rhueandsymone

Kiss of Life: https://geni.us/cameronandtara

Kiss of Fate : https://geni.us/Rayandnicole

Kiss of Karma: https://geni.us/Richardandkeisha

THE CHESAPEAKE HEIGHTS SERIES

Free to Fall: https://geni.us/FreetoFall

Free to Crave: https://geni.us/Freetocrave

STAND-ALONE NOVELS & NOVELLAS

Savannah's Salvation: https://geni.us/MichaelandSavannah

The Wine Down: https://geni.us/RiddickandBrandi

Love & Lipstick: https://geni.us/PeterandMia

Love & Lyrics: https://geni.us/LukerandRaina

Make Me:https://geni.us/MakeMeSir

ABOUT THE AUTHOR

ABOUT LOUISE LENNOX

Contemporary romance Author Louise Lennox is a hopeful romantic writing steamy romances full of heart and healing.

A Spelman College and Georgetown University graduate, Louise provides women with diverse and meaningful representation in romance novel pages. Not seeing enough women like herself headlining positive love stories, she launched #HappyBlackRomance; a community of readers and writers committed to creating and sharing positive romance stories featuring Black heroines.

Louise Lennox plots highlight the joys of Black relationships across the diaspora, pushing readers from all cultural backgrounds to admire them for their strength and downright sexiness. In her novels, sparks always fly; the sex amazes, and the characters always leave the world better than they found it through their love.

When she's not writing, Louise is enjoying her work as a school leader, wife, and mother of the two cutest dragons ever to walk the earth!

To learn more about #HappyBlackRomance and to score a free book or two, check out her website www.lovelouiselennox.com.

www.ingramcontent.com/pod-product-compliance
Lightning Source LLC
Chambersburg PA
CBHW020631260626
47157CB00008B/2693